MISPLACED

BRITTNI BRINN

Misplaced
Brittni Brinn

This is a work of fiction. **Any similarity to actual persons, living, dead, undead, or actual events is purely coincidental.**

@littleghostsboo 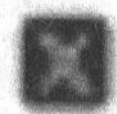

@littleghostsbooks 

Published by Little Ghosts Books.
Visit us at littleghostsbooks.com

Little Ghosts Books is committed to protecting the environment. The entirety of this book, the cover as well as the interior, is printed on acid-free 100% recycled fibers within Canada.

First Ed. 11.01.2024

Cover Designed and illustrated by Chris Krawczyk.

Edited by Chris Krawczyk & phillip rowan

ISBN: 978-1-7389097-6-6

*For the Supina family
and all of the Concordia kids*

Misplaced

CHAPTER ONE
Mouth

SOME LADY LEFT her mouth in the mall bathroom. Crumpled up in a napkin next to the stainless-steel soap dispenser. I almost ignore it—but then I think, Christ, what if she were me and I needed to say something? If I were biting into a sandwich, or at the front desk for a dental appointment? I'd need a mouth for something like that.

I wipe my hands on my jeans and fold the napkin around the mouth before sliding it into my pocket. Rushing after the mouth's owner, I side-step the swinging bathroom door, head through the mall's dingy entryway, and out into the street. The scuffed glass door whooshes shut behind me.

She's already a block down the sidewalk. Keeping my pace steady to avoid damaging the piece in my pocket, I follow, the bright cold forcing a squint-view.

"Wait up!" I call, loudly enough.

She keeps walking. Maybe she's misplaced her ears as well—it's difficult to tell with the floppy toque she's got on, bright red with a navy blue pom-pom. Her eccentric fit continues with a faded shawl wrapped over an old, beige trench coat. Old pants too, the brown cuffs worn down to grey at the heels.

I trail her all the way down Tendon Street, past the rusty chain-link caging the bricked-up school, past the *High Five Boutique* with its delicate hands positioned coyly in the window. Some wear white button-up gloves, some have painted fingernails. The grease-soaked smell from the burger joint next door fills my nose, but I rush past, thinking more about the empty mouth in my pocket than my own.

The mouth's owner waits at the corner, scuffing at the curb with a rubber-soled hiking boot.

"Hey!" I'm close enough now to put a hand on her shoulder.

Her arrow-sharp profile remains fixed towards the DON'T WALK sign. Red light flashes across the smooth patch of dark brown skin between her nose and chin—where a mouth should be and definitely isn't.

"I think this is yours." I take the napkin square from my pocket, hold it out to her.

Her eyes snap to mine, greying eyebrows digging into the bridge of her nose, thin nostrils flaring slightly. She knocks my hand away and strides across the street.

"No, wait!" She must've forgotten, I reason as I run. Probably thinks I'm trying to scam her, sell her some grimy spare part.

She mounts the fire escape stairs tacked to the side of a brick apartment block.

"You, on the stairs!" I shout, about to give up. "You left your mouth, your *mouth*, in the bathroom! It's wrapped up, here!" I raise my hand, offering the napkin in my palm.

She pauses. Turns from the door, keys dangling from her left hand. Her fingers explore the lower half of her face. Realization widens her eyes. She motions me up with the keys as she disappears into the building.

I could leave the mouth on the railing, head back to the cold bus shelter behind the mall, but I've come too far to risk it getting swiped by some alley walker or chewed up by a hungry stray.

And...something draws me forward, a sense of urgency—a sharp fingernail pointing directly at the stranger's door.

My shoes clang up the dimpled stairs, the metal sharp under my thin plastic soles. I pass through the apartment's open door and shut it behind me.

The stranger waits in the entryway, framed by two racks overstuffed with coats. Layers of winter boots, runners, and dress shoes line the scuffed hardwood underneath. She removes her oversized toque to reveal short white hair washed upwards, a rogue strand plastered diagonally across her narrow forehead.

I hand the napkin over. Toque under one arm, she unfolds the square and works her short fingers underneath the mouth, placing it between her chin and nose. It slides slightly—holds.

"God-fucking-dammit!" the mouth exclaims and snaps shut. She works the mouth muscles to make sure the connection is good, lips opening it in a wide, silent *wow*.

"You're an odd one, aren't you?" Her voice warms as she turns her attention to me. "Chasing a stranger down the street to return a mouth? You could've sold it, you know. Not for much, but every little bit helps. Jessica Fit."

Pulling back the loose trench coat sleeve, she offers her hand. Strong grip, deliberate shake, one-two, up-down.

"I'm Nan."

"I owe you, Nan." She frees her hand to press down the corner of her mouth. "Can I make you a coffee?"

I follow her into a barely furnished living room. A folded-up plastic table leans against the wall next to a deck chair with a missing slat. The space above is packed full of paintings, frames close enough to give each other slivers. Thin winter light washes through the sliding balcony door over a striped area rug.

The only other fixture of the room is a heavy-set figure sitting cross-legged in the corner. Lips pout from her otherwise blank face. Eyes, nose, eyebrows—they're laid out in a neat line on a scrap of cloth in front of her.

"Meditating," Jessica Fit explains as she knocks one of the picture frames slightly to the left. "She keeps her ears on, to show her 'openness to the universe'."

"What about her mouth?" I ask.

Jessica quirks an eyebrow. "That's so she can breathe." She stands back to appraise the painting of a square-shaped man wearing a bowler hat.

Some of the paintings are like nothing I've ever seen before; faces with noses askew, mouths balancing on their ends, eyes melting into cheek wells. I feel myself becoming unmoored, lost in the chaotic jumble. What if the spots for body parts actually moved around like that? How the hell would we know where anything was supposed to go?

A siren whines through the apartment. Jessica takes a clunky cell phone out of her pocket and cancels the alarm without looking. "Rise and shine, Reena!"

Reena...

The name leaves an unpleasant ringing in my ears, echoes through the dark places and settles deep in my gut like a shard of ice. I shudder as the faceless, foreboding person in the corner begins to move.

Reena resets her left eye. She plucks the other eyeball from the cloth and holds it to where the socket should be. There's a slight *shhhk* as the eye settles into place. The dread of Reena's presence rises as she stands, her face complete.

"Are you sure you don't fall asleep during these things?" Jessica teases on her way over to the kitchen.

Reena's lower lip protrudes, a mouth too small for her round adult face. The rest of her features are where they should be—thick black eyebrows, a wide-bridged nose. She hits me with a blue-eyed glare that rivals the temperature outside. The pout deepens to a frown.

"Do you take cream or sugar?" Jessica shouts from around the corner.

Desperate to escape Reena's sightline, I follow Jessica's voice. A long arm of countertop with barstools tucked underneath separates the open-concept kitchen from the rest of the apartment. Jessica drapes her trench coat over the counter, the toque's pom-pom sticking out from the pocket. Across the divide, the kitchen is chaos and clutter: herb pots fill the windowsill above a double sink; jars of pasta, flour, and other baking supplies crowd the back counter; a lazy susan packed with spices sits beside the electric stove; photos and drawings and scribbled notes coat the fridge.

Completely at home, Jessica sets two handmade mugs on the countertop between us.

"Black coffee for me," I say.

Jessica slides the half-full glass pot from under the coffeemaker and pours. "I'd make a fresh batch but you've caught us on our busiest day." She turns one of the mugs towards me so that the handle is in easy reach.

"Doesn't seem like it."

Jessica stirs a spoonful of creamer into her mug. "Reena and I both needed to clear our heads before the rush. Did you see the coats when you came in?"

"There's a lot of them."

"We're expecting a lot of folks to come by wanting one." She refers to the digital clock on the stove. "In about fifteen minutes."

I sip the coffee. The dark roast has a bittersweet aftertaste. "Do you need help?"

"Are you sure?" Jessica studies me over her mug. "You've already gone out of your way."

"I literally have nowhere else to be."

"Well," she smiles, "we can definitely use the extra set of hands."

CHAPTER TWO
Pinky

REENA SWINGS THE chair from against the wall, pretty much throwing it towards the coat-lined entryway. It tips forward, lurches back, legs skidding a couple steps before managing to break the inertia. She glances at me. "That's for you."

My gut bursting with coffee, I sit in line with the door frame separating the entryway and the bare living room. Reena snaps the plastic table open in front of me, so low it presses down on my thighs.

"The chair is offended," Reena tells me.

"Umm?"

"It doesn't like you."

I turn in the seat, study the back of it. The second slat is missing. The empty space curves downwards in a frown. As I start to get up, my inner exit light flashing urgently, she shakes her head.

"It's resigned itself to a working relationship. Just don't piss it off."

Low tabletop pressing on my thighs. Offended chair pressing into my spine. Reena's glacial glare freezing me in place. What am I even doing here?

Jessica places a two-litre canning jar at my elbow, her welcoming smile cutting through Reena's disapproval. "Thanks for agreeing to stay. I'll be on shoes, Reena will be on coats. If you could ask each person for their sizes, that would really help. If people want to give a donation, that's what the jar's for. Here we go!" Then, without any further direction, she opens the front door.

Outside, the fire escape landing is packed with faces that squiggle and crowd like cells under a microscope. Many of them are shivering, with running noses, harrowed eyes, and greasy lines of hair dripping down their foreheads.

"A large winter coat," says the first, placing a holey windbreaker on the table and dropping a handful of silver change into the jar. Reena unhooks a padded evergreen jacket from the rack and the person nods, only a hint of warmth on their grizzled face.

They're all here to trade in; some for coats, some for shoes, most for both. Person after person after person. They approach the table from their place in line at the door, patient until they come up to us, most with worry around their eyes. Worry for themselves, their families, the future? I can recognize it, but only through a fog. There are so many. I lose count, asking for sizes, watching the faces.

One face stands out. One with a markless complexion. Not that he's acne-free or anything—his skin has no colour. Not obsidian, not sand, not porcelain, not copper, not amber, not brown, not beige. Not tan. Not black. Not white. His skin is see-through without being clear. It's hard to describe and even more difficult to look at. I find my gaze sliding off him, beads of water on Teflon.

He waits at the back of the entryway until the multitude have left with their new coats and shoes. Then, he comes up to me. "One of each, please."

As if already expecting his request, Reena sets the last coat and the last pair of shoes on the table: a thick brown tweed, knee-length with three black buttons, and red rubber boots lined with sheep wool.

The coat he's taken off—puffy purple, the zipper pull replaced by a rusted safety pin—slips from the mound of coats behind me, water-resistant shell shhhhing to the floor. He folds the new coat in half and hangs it over the top shelf of the empty coat rack.

A washed-out grey hoodie hangs loose past his waist. What looks like nurse's scrub pants underneath, beach tan with bulky velcroed-shut pockets. He takes off his socks—revealing bony feet with a jumble of white lint caught on the ragged edge of his big toenail—and lays them next to his new boots.

He catches me looking at his feet and starts laughing, a rolling and clear sound like a boat engine early in the morning. "I'll be back in a minute," he says to Jessica. Still laughing, he navigates the marsh of coats strewn over the living room floor and disappears into the narrow hallway at the back of the apartment.

"That's Adam," Jessica Fit tells me with a thoughtful nod. "He's back early."

Reena starts emptying coat pockets. Whatever shit she finds ends up on the table next to the half-full jar of spare change. Jessica stands next to me, sorting. Screwed-up Kleenex, candy wrappers, and crumpled receipts drop into the garbage bag at her feet. Loose coinage into the jar. Packs of gum, cigarettes, unscratched lottery tickets, single gloves, and lighters get thrown into a cardboard shoebox.

"Sitting around?" Reena glowers at me, a stained suit jacket in her hands. The jacket has a ripped lapel and a grease stain the size of a ham across the stomach.

In a near panic, I scurry to the mountain of coats and grab a pink windbreaker. I go through the pockets: a handful of thick elastic bands, two latex gloves, a roll of hockey tape, and a condom (packaged).

Jessica nods as I dump them in front of her. Her hand sweeps everything into the garbage bag. "You don't have to stay, y'know. This part can get a bit tedious."

Reena stuffs a jean jacket into a clear plastic garbage bag, pressing the stained suit deeper underneath.

"What happens to it all?" I ask.

"We empty them. Wash them. Fix them. Then we do this," Jessica motions to the table and the front door, conjuring the microscope slide of unwashed faces, "all again."

I drop the emptied windbreaker into a new bag. "Seems like a lot of work. What do you get out of it, besides a million gross coats and like $10 in change?"

She shrugs. "Clothes usually get thrown out by the dumpster loads. So, we reuse what we can, fix them up, and give them away."

Trying to ignore the reek rising from the pile, I grab another jacket. "What about the really beat-up ones?"

Jessica leans forward, motioning me closer with a subtle flick of her eyes. "Reena can do anything with a sewing machine. I don't know where she learned, but she's talented. She has an eye for seams." Jessica moves back, tossing a golf pencil and three matchbooks into the keep box. "Shoes, those are a different story. Those we leave to Mr. Snaff."

"Jessica? Found something." Reena appears next to me, a finger lying across her palm. It's a pinky finger, the dot of nail painted sparkly purple.

We all stare at it, completely silent. The finger is too small, too round, too soft to belong to an adult. The taste of bile rises up my oesophagus, but I manage to push down the nausea. If it's a child's finger, it's a child who hit puberty early—the end of the digit is rounded, whole. No blood. Still, it's disturbing. What the hell was someone doing with a kid's finger in their pocket?

Jessica Fit is the first to speak. "If no one claims it by tomorrow, we'll take it to the hospital."

Reena's hand closes protectively around the pinky finger. "It's scared," she says, adult disgust on her juvenile lips. Her frown leaves a deep fissure in the air as she moves into the kitchen.

In the silence that follows, I feel an opening to leave. It gapes—and passes.

CHAPTER THREE
Eyelids

"YOU'RE LOOKING WELL, Adam." Jessica moves around the kitchen counter, balancing four full mugs, two in each hand, and a bowl of sugar wedged into the crook of her elbow. Everything makes it to the rug serving as our table and chairs, not a drop or granule less.

Reena pouts into the mug Jessica sets in front of her. Seemingly satisfied by the green tea inside, she cups her hands around it.

"Thanks, Mom." Adam scoops four heaping teaspoons of sugar into his mug of coffee. "Looks like you've found a new assistant." He sends a friendly smile my way.

"Without Nan I wouldn't be drinking this coffee right now. They've been a great help. Drink some of that, don't be shy," Jessica nods at me, *another cup, have another.*

Inside my stomach is a sloshing sea of black caffeine, but I'm not one to refuse free coffee.

I've been here for hours, I don't know how long exactly. The hundreds of coats are packed inside clear garbage bags heaped against the wall at the back of the apartment. Boxes of worn-out shoes hold the plastic avalanche at bay. The stained suit jacket faces me, pressed up against the inside of its full bag. I wonder who wore it. I wonder what they're wearing now.

"… so Bodhidharma cut off his eyelids." Reena takes a sip of tea, her ice-blue eyes briefly obscured in close-eyed contentment. Her body, so powerful, a force simply in its presence, is now relaxed, cross-legged.

"I have a question," Adam says.

She nods.

"Why did Bodhidharma cut off his eyelids instead of just removing them while he was meditating? Why throw them away? It's not like he could just grow another set."

"He was a passionate person. He was furious about giving into his physical needs while he was pursuing a spiritual end. So, he did something drastic."

"But can't sleeping be a path to enlightenment as well? What about revelatory dreams?"

A growl rises in Reena's throat. "I'm not saying that what he did was the only answer."

Adam takes a sip of coffee. "Let me ask one more thing—honestly, I find this story very interesting—so people use the daruma doll, which is based on Bodhidharma, for wishing. And when the wish comes true, or the goal is attained, they paint in the second eye and eventually burn the doll to signify distance from worldly wealth or success—"

"I can see where you're going, Adam."

"—but why have those desires or wishes in the first place, and why try to fulfil them? Aren't desires inherently against what Bodhidharma stands for?"

A pouting frown reinstates itself on her face. "It's true that we shouldn't become attached to worldly things, because the world doesn't last. Only the spiritual endures. But—" her eyelids lift, the lines in her face soften, "you already believe that."

Adam grins in reply. It's more than a simple line change: the smile spreads through his whole face, like dye in water. When I try to determine the colour, I find myself looking at the painting of the bowler hat man instead.

"I have to apologise for my son and Reena," Jessica says, on the verge of laughter. "They're always like this."

"Like what?" I ask. They're too many things to be like one thing.

"They forget that there are other people in the room."

"That's not true," Adam responds. "I am very aware."

Reena shrugs. "Anyone who can handle our banter won't be scared off when they really get to know us. You're not scared, are you?"

I shake my head, maybe too quickly.

"Reena's a great sage," Adam says to me, a hint of comfort in his voice. His eyelids droop slightly, like he's tired but trying not to look it.

"Pshh," Reena brushes the compliment off with a frown.

"I admire her, very much." His voice lowers with sincerity.

Reena's eyes narrow. "Your—your hair is very friendly."

Adam accepts the comment with another sip of coffee. Seems he's used to Reena's weird way of talking.

"How are you all related anyway?" I cut in.

Jessica reaches for another spoonful of sugar. "None of us are."

"You just said Adam was your son."

"I consider him my son. But we're not at all related, not by blood."

The three of them smile at each other, as if sharing a joke.

"What does that mean?"

Adam sits back on his heels, his hands braced on the tan knees of his scrub pants. "When I was seven years old, I had no family, nothing much else either. I was walking down this street, by chance, on the day Jessica was giving away coats. She asked me to stay and help her empty pockets. After that, I lived here and she took care of me."

"That's out of a book," I say. "Dickens, or something."

"There's a lot to be said about coincidence," Jessica nods. "At the time, I was tired of the coats and was considering giving up. But Adam convinced me: if people need something that I can give, I have no excuse for not giving it."

"I guess we met by coincidence too," I venture, the beckoning exit light in my brain fading to black.

"That's why I asked you to stay. You followed me, trying to help someone you had no reason to. So, who's to say there isn't another reason you're here? Why don't you join us for supper?"

Reena finishes her tea. She places the mug down and stares into emptiness, legs crossed, her blue eyes holding open, far away.

"Why not?" I take another sip of coffee.

CHAPTER FOUR
No Neck

THE INSIDE OF my elbows ache from boxes of shoes and boots carried down the fire escape to the chipper orange sedan. It sports mismatched tires and a rusty tailpipe. The passenger side window is held up with a paint stick and three long strips of masking tape.

Mr. Polonious Snaff re-enters the living room after me, eyebrows arched all the way to his weak hairline, breathing heavily through his teeth.

"That's the last of them, Jess!" he announces.

How all of the boxes fit into his piece-of-shit car will forever remain a mystery. I stretch my arms across my chest, shake out my sore hands. I'm tempted to remove them, just to get a break, but the aching pain would just be there when I reattach them, so I deal.

"I should be on my way! Still have a stack of last week's quizzes to grade!" Mr. Snaff reaches into his pocket for an honest-to-god cloth handkerchief. With polka dots.

Jessica doesn't miss a beat. "Stay for supper, at least."

Wiping the sweat from his forehead, Mr. Snaff lets out a sigh. "You know I would love to, Jess, but the work is never through!"

"Please. As a thank you for taking on all those poor *soles*."

"Ah-ha! Jess, sharp as ever! Well, of course, when you put it so nicely! I'll stay." Mr. Snaff has a big voice and whenever he talks his mouth stretches widely side to side to accommodate, since his chin has nowhere else to go—he barely has a neck. Lots of stuffy, old teachers seem to be in this club, the No Neck Club. Like necks are for the uneducated.

But Mr. Snaff isn't the stuffy type, not really. His hands are comical, the size of pancakes and the same colour, with longer fingers than you would expect from a guy of his roundness. He should really just get the hospital to install a new neck 'cause his head is angled way back so that he has to look down his nose to really see you. But the thing is, he's delighted with whatever he sees past the end of his nose, and delighted is the opposite of stuffy.

The low table is cleared of the coin jar and the box of odd ends. A faded tablecloth patterned with intertwining leaves and purple birds takes their place. Forks, knives, glasses, plates—Adam and Reena set the table at an amazing speed, bringing side dishes of broccoli and quinoa and a glass jug of lemonade. Jessica carries in a covered serving dish with oven mitts, placing it, steaming, in the middle of the low table.

Caught up in the smell of food and the emptiness of my own body, I almost forget to sit down. A wooden bench and three chairs have materialised from the recesses of the apartment. Adam and Reena share the bench. Jessica sits on the edge of the chair with the missing slat. Mr. Snaff relaxes into his seat and

I take the last folding chair on his left. A moment of silence follows, and then, finally, we eat.

Between bites of what tastes like the best food I've ever had, I glance up at Adam and Reena. They're around the same age, a few years older than me. Even sitting down, Adam is a full foot and a half taller than Reena. Her gold-brown skin almost glows in comparison with his literally colourless complexion. The icy dread of Reena's presence is dampened by Adam's calm, sparse figure and tired eyes.

Adam helps himself to another scoop of potatoes as Reena reaches for the bowl of quinoa. Their hands collide. Their eyes meet quickly and slide away. They both apologise.

Adam becomes engrossed with flattening his mashed potatoes, and Reena gets up, taking the empty glass pitcher to the sink.

Mr. Snaff lifts a forkful of rosemary chicken to his upturned nose and sniffs. "Superb!" he exclaims, completing the utensil's trajectory. The four-pronged fork slides from his mouth, immaculate.

Jessica's resulting smile is sharply affectionate; as if her dinner guest is a younger brother or a favourite nephew, not an eccentric school teacher who fixes shoes for a hobby.

Reena sets a full pitcher of water on the table and sits as far from Adam as their shared bench will allow.

"What're you teaching this year, Mr. Snaff?" Adam's on his second helping of chicken, mostly 'cause he's been talking the least. Well, apart from me. I finished my plate ages ago.

"Biology and Health! Remember those, Adam? You wouldn't dissect the pig foetus, as I recall!" He laughs in a bantering sort of way that tells me it's a story often told in this circle. "You asked if you could take apart a pinecone instead! How detailed your report was! I'm surprised to this day that you didn't become a botanist!"

Adam smiles quietly, looking at Mr. Snaff with that same family-like affection.

"Yes, Biology is a treat, though Health is less so! Telling teenagers to avoid unprotected genital trading, that is not my idea of a good time! But, understood, it must be done, and all the staff rotate, so really one year out of three isn't bad, is it? Quite fair!" If he had a neck, he'd be nodding right now. As it is, his chin juts slightly and returns, relaxing into the open collar of his butter yellow shirt. "Any chance for more broccoli, Jess?"

"Of course! There's plenty." She moves to the kitchen like a hawk reeling from one cliff to another.

"And how about you, my dear!" Mr. Polonious Snaff turns his face—well, his whole torso—towards me. I have his full attention.

"How about me, what?"

"Where," his free hand circles some vague location in the air, "where do you fit into all of this madness!"

"Nowhere, really. I was just…" I look over to Reena, but her face may as well be blank, "helping out today."

"How wonderful! Are you a student? I haven't taught you before, have I? If that's the case, you'll have to forgive me—"

"I don't go to school." It surprises me as I say it, but it must be true. I haven't been to school in a long time.

"So, you're older than you look, are you! Employed, then? I bet you're working at some kind of, whatchacallit—"

"In the downtown shopping centre. I sell sunglasses."

"Oh really! Do you have any interest in shoes?"

I swallow a sip of lemonade to dull the panic these questions are causing. "Not really."

"That's a shame! A darned shame!"

Jessica appears at his shoulder, placing a mountain of steamed broccoli next to his plate. "That's all that's left. Please help yourself."

Mr. Snaff spreads his hands. "Would anyone else desire some of this delightful member of the cabbage family?"

"Me, thanks," Reena takes him up on the offer. "The cabbage family?"

"Oh yes! Specially developed through selective growth!" Mr. Snaff scoops a stalk and gleefully transfers it onto her plate.

"Mr. Snaff, I've been reading about synthetic body parts," Adam segues, maybe to prove he's not as interested in plants as he used to be. "Some articles are saying that once they figure out how to extend the lifetime of a part, they can also expect novelty parts to be accepted with almost 100% regularity."

Jessica shakes her head. "I've read about that, too. They're still trying to figure out what keeps the body parts together, how and why they bond and detach according to a subject's response. You know, with completely synthetic parts, sometimes the connection doesn't hold. An arm will fall off mid-swing, lips will drip down the face, toes will be found between bed sheets. Compatibility doesn't seem to ensure attachment. Even passion is no assurance."

The mouthful of lemonade goes sour in my mouth. A low pang spreads through my right hand and returns to the dark places, like a single note struck on a deep iron bell. Doomed ships and foghorns rise up in my mind. I grip my hand into a fist under the table. Release it.

"No assurance whatsoever!" Mr. Snaff agrees. "This is what I stress in my Health classes." He *tsks* and tips his torso from side to side as he spears another tree of broccoli.

Supper comes to an end. Adam clears the dishes. We eat canned peaches for dessert. Mr. Polonious Snaff exits with a grand "Goodnight to all!" and Reena picks up one of the folding chairs and disappears down the back hallway.

It's getting late. There's a faint blinking in my inner darkness, a reminder of where the door is and how to leave.

"Are you okay to make it home?" Jessica asks as she and Adam walk me to the entryway. "I hope it's not too far."

"I'm good."

"Thanks again," she says, holding out her hand. "And you're always welcome. Truly."

"Okay." I watch my arm as her strong grip moves it up and down.

I'm halfway down the fire escape when Adam calls down from the door, "Hey, don't you have a coat?"

No, I remember. Just the double layer of sweaters I wore to work. So I shrug, my hands balled up in the worsted cotton pockets.

He goes back inside, leaving the door open. I've already left the party and waiting on the stairs seems silly, but as I start back downwards, the pebbled metal shakes underfoot and Adam appears next to me. He holds out the tweed coat with three back buttons. The coat he traded in for.

"It's freezing out here," he says, clear eyes insisting I take it.

So I push my arms into the sleeves, shrugging it over my shoulders. It smells of industrial detergent and laundromat washers. The hem brushes my calves. "I'll bring it back," I mumble as my fingers secure the buttons.

"If you don't, it's no problem. But I hope we see you again." Even in the faint light spilling down from the open doorway, I can see the smile diffuse across his face.

"Thanks." I take the rest of the stairs casually, but as soon as I hear the apartment door close, I look back, finding one of their bright windows in the dark.

INTERLUDE ONE:
Reena's Mouth
Ten Years Previous

DARK. COLD. HURTS.

Try not to let my eyes cry. They are sad. They are sad because there is pain. I clench my hands but the biting pains do not stop.

Faint light. Outline of the single chair with folded clothes on the seat. The Father left the door open. He didn't lock it. A strip of yellow torn from the wall of black.

I have a sheet. I am laying on it, it is thin, and I hurt—

Don't think about it. Not supposed to think about it.

In ten seconds, I will get up.

One.

Two—

I will go over to the chair.

Three—

And put on the skirt and blouse. There are no shoes.

Four.

Five—

Where can I find shoes?

Six—

Hurts—

Seven—

The sheet will wrap around me like a coat.

Eight, Nine—

Bright rush confuses my eyes. I am sitting up. Deep breaths. The room focuses.

Bare feet, cold stone floor. Fabric hugs my body. Fully dressed now.

I lift the sheet from the mattress on the floor. Saggy mattress on the floor, I feel sorry for you.

I curl myself around the open door, look both ways. No one in the halls. Cavernous and fully lit. It's an old stone building with colourful glass in the windows. Some people think it's beautiful. That's what one of the Mothers says, though not with her mouth. We're not allowed to say useless things like that.

No one in the halls. Be quiet feet, you're so clumsy, like two big trolls banging on the floor.

My aching hands gather the sheet around me, closer, so close I can feel its belly rumble. It is so thin, it has not eaten anything in forever. It is so thin. But it doesn't have a mouth. There is no way to feed it.

The door to this room is open, too. There is only darkness inside, crouching. Darkness is always crouching.

If I am quiet enough, it will not jump at me.

I close my eyes. Wait for the darkness to creep and crouch around me.

Open my eyes. The back wall is covered in shelves. On the shelves, there are jars. They look cold. All of them not touching, set apart from each other.

Where is mine?

I picture where I placed it after mealtime yesterday. Fourth from the left on the bottom row. That's it. That's where—

Echoing footsteps in the hallway. Approaching. Louder and louder.

Please, don't find me here.

Trolls eat little girls.

Stomp on their bones.

My hands hurt—

Big shadow in the doorway. His eyes adjusting, will he turn on the—

"What the hell are you doing in here?"

The light has wings, beating at my eyes. The light flies away. It leaves me behind.

"I won't ask again."

But I can't say why. I *can't.*

The Brother with the short brown hair and moustache goes over to the shelf. "Did you come all the way out here for this?" His proud fingers point at the fourth jar from the left on the bottom row. "You know that being in this room is a sin!"

There is nothing to me now. He will tear up the sheet, and tell the Father what I've done.

"The other Mothers will be ashamed of you, Maria."

Flash of all the Mothers, standing in line at the stone table, each receiving their mouth for mealtime—

"Come now," his words are bristling, wild dogs as he comes towards me, "time for bed."

Arrogant hands close around my waist, he's about to lift me, oh no, not my sheet, it's so thin, don't hurt it—

"Bitch!"

I'm on the floor now. His hand covers where his mean eye is. My knuckles ache from striking the wall of his angry cheek.

"You listen to me," he looms overhead. "You're going back to your room."

He's going to kick me, this one always kicks me. I roll away. The sheet comes loose, I pull it fast after me, pulling it free from under his heavy feet—

A yell. A heavy crack. A moan.

Still, be still, don't move.

He is silent, out of sight, no longer moaning.

Shh, it's okay, sheet. I'll find a way to feed you.

The Brother doesn't move.

The darkness crouches underneath the shelf, rolled in dust.

The fourth jar from the left.

Hard, cool glass, protecting what's inside.

I unscrew the lid.

I scoop up the mouth.

It feels familiar. My face welcomes it.

Come with me, sheet. We have a long way to go tonight.

The body on the floor is still.

"Goodbye."

I said it. I have said it. I have said it forever.

CHAPTER FIVE
Beauty Mark

BEAUTY MARK IS JUST two blocks from Jessica Fit's place. They always have a good mix playing: Beat, Electronika, and Analog throwbacks. Plus, it's always full. Enough people to fill all the spaces, no room for questions, no room for anything else.

A short line-up of people waits along the stuccoed building. Heavy beats pump through the wall. The person in front of me is already wasted, hanging off their date's shoulder, their elongated neck bare and drooping.

Luckily, it's a weekday; on a Saturday, there'd be no chance of getting in, not dressed like this. I took off Adam's oversized coat before getting in line, but my knitted sweater is bulky, not sexy at all. My jeans look tired from the long day at the Fits's —I don't know what else to call the place, and oh my god, I'm thinking like Reena. No way my jeans are actually tired.

"Birthdate?" the bouncer at the door asks me. "Birthname?" A tag pinned to his tight black v-neck reads *Basil, he/him*. His eyes are deep set, as if someone shot two heavy silver bullets at him and they got wedged there in his skull. He obviously switches out his usual eyes to intimidate the people coming in, staring them down with those oversized metal marbles.

A hand that could crush my skull returns my ID card. He motions me through the sleek black doors with gold-plated handles. Music explodes into me. My feet carry me around the low square tables and velvet booths until I reach the bar.

"Vodka tonic, tall!" I tell the bartender.

The music's too loud, but the best bartenders can read minds. "Right on, sweet thing!" They wink, the club's namesake above the right corner of their lip. Their eyelashes are long enough to eclipse their manicured eyebrows. How many foreheads do they have at home, which one do they wear grocery shopping?

Keeping an elbow on the bar, I scan the dancefloor. The pack of arms, legs, flashes of teeth, and bare torsos bounce to the Neon-Techno. Something tugs at me, a face I think I recognize, lost in the crowd—

The bartender places a clear glass on the bartop. "There ya go!"

"THANKS!" I'm talking too loud, even for here. I wonder what voice I would buy if I decided I hated mine.

The tall glass is the only answer I need, cool against my fingers. I turn to find a place to settle in for the night—

"Hey! Honey!" The bartender leans towards me, their hand on my arm so delicate. "That one over there. Sunglasses. See?"

"Yeah?" He's sitting at one of the booths with three others; a square-jawed guy and a petite brunette with three eyes. The third person's face is hidden in the shadowed corner of the booth.

The bartender shakes their head and pulls their voice down as low as it can go in the noise. "Might want to avoid him."

"I've been here before, you know! I can take care of—"

"Just a warning—he's trouble. I've been telling all the young—"

"I'm old enough, alright? Christ!" I move out of their reach, my hand around the vodka tonic.

I try to shake off the sense of foreboding as I weave between tables. Is management trying to weed out minors or something? Doesn't matter. Besides, I just walked by the booth and the guy wearing sunglasses didn't even notice.

Here's a table. Soft seat. Vibrations from the floor stamping up my legs, shaking the glass. I'll finish this one then lose myself—

"What's a cute thing like you doing sitting alone?" It's the square-jawed guy from the booth, standing there all trendy in a paisley button-down shirt, charcoal shorts, and square-toed dress shoes, hair gathered in a bun on the top of his head. I hate to admit it, but the button nose, super popular right now, looks good on him.

"I'm Cameron. Want to join us?" He juts his chin at the sunglassed man, the three-eyed brunette, and the shadowed face in the corner.

I hold up my hands palms outwards and shake my head, hoping he'll settle for a polite refusal.

"You don't have to sit by yourself! Come on, it'll be fun!"

"I want to be alone! There's no law against that, is there?"

"I think you'd really like it—"

"Listen!"—take the hint, buddy—"I have every right to be here! And drink alone! And in peace!"

"Fine," he says in a huff. "I'm supposed to give this to you, anyway."

He digs into his pocket and takes out a bag, the kind you get at eco-friendly gift shops. The brown paper is stamped with a blue-ink outline of a hand. When I don't move to take it, he drops the bag on the table. It teeters a moment from the weight at the bottom and tips towards me. Inside the crumpled paper mouth—purple glitter. A flash of flesh.

I'm afraid to look up even though I know Cameron's gone back to the booth. Keeping my expression neutral, I frantically come up with an exit plan. I'll finish my drink, throw the bag back in his face, and run for the door. By the time I gather the courage to glance over at his table, it's empty.

A resounding hum threads through my right hand. Bile clamours up my throat, but I keep it contained. The *High Five Hand Boutique* logo on the bag distorts as I tip my glass and watch it shiver through the alcohol.

CHAPTER SIX
Ring

THE NEXT AFTERNOON, I take the bag and the remnants of a hangover to the Fits's apartment.

The brown paper crinkles as Jessica uncurls the top of the bag. She tips it over so the prepubescent finger inside rolls out onto the kitchen counter. Purple sparkles coat the fingernail.

It's obvious: the ring finger is from the same hand as yesterday's pinky.

Jessica's mouth makes a firm line, her eyebrows pressing deep into the bridge of her nose. "Reena's just taken the little one to the hospital."

Little one, like it's a sick child. "A guy gave it to me last night. Said he was supposed to deliver it or something."

Jessica's sharp nose lifts as if she's just passed an open dumpster. "Distributing a sample of his...product."

"But it's the same kid, the one losing all these fingers."

"Seems that way."

"Fingers can look the same. Or maybe they're grown in test tubes. That's how they make synthetic parts, right?"

Jessica shakes her head and states the obvious. "There's no point developing them for children that young."

Like a layer of film placed over a running reel, I remember my first time.

I was thirteen. Sitting by a river, on a family trip somewhere. Low, blue-grey thunderheads, an electric smell charging the air. Knees drawn up, supporting my chin. Fidgeting with my right earlobe, waiting for the storm to cross the river with crashing voices. That's when I felt it peeling off into my hand, taking stereo with it. Leaving me with only one side of the story.

I'd never really seen my ear that closely before. Flat in my palm, it could've been the start of a spiral maze, around and down into a dark tunnel, deep through the back of my hand and into the earth.

I held it tight to the side of my head all the way back to the campground, afraid it would come off and get lost in the tall grass.

Mom was reading in a blue and yellow striped lawn chair. I climbed over her book and whispered into her ear what had happened.

"You don't have to be scared," she whispered back, "It's a very natural part of growing up." She swept back the golden curtain of her hair and removed her ear. A simple silver leaf earring dangled from it. I reached for that same feeling and held my ear up to her, proud that I was old enough for whatever this was.

But when I look at the small, purple-nailed finger on the kitchen counter, I don't get that feeling at all. I hate to admit it, but Reena was right: there's definitely something sad about these disembodied fingers.

Jessica turns the paper bag over. A look of pure rage watersheds down her face when she sees the logo. "*Marius.*"

"Who's th—?"

"But why? Why the—Why the f—!" Jessica's fingers fly to her mouth and start to peel it off.

"You know him?" I interrupt.

Jessica crumples the empty bag. She closes her eyes and presses her mouth back into place. "Yes." When she opens her eyes again, the torrent of anger has settled into a deep, seething pool. She shakes her head slightly. Her hands smooth the bag out and gently deposit the finger back inside.

I take the break in conversation to shrug off the tweed jacket. "Is Adam here? I wanted to give this back to him." Hopefully, I glance down the back hallway, but all the doors are closed.

"He's running some errands," Jessica says, then looks up. "He lent you this one? Do you need a coat?"

The question surprises me. "Yeah, actually. I've just been wearing sweaters." It's the middle of winter, for Christ's sake. Why *don't* I have a jacket? I must've lost it, maybe left it at work or something.

"We put half a dozen decent ones through the wash this morning. They're on the entryway rack. Take your pick." Jessica's gaze goes to the paintings across the apartment. "And then, I'm going to *High Five* to get some answers."

"I'll go with you," I try to sound confident. "I'd like some answers too. Like, why that slimeball singled me out last night. What's with these fingers anyway? If it's a marketing scheme, it's pretty fucked up, right?"

A ripple of anger passes over Jessica's face. "With Marius, everything is."

CHAPTER SEVEN
Amber's High Five

HIGH FIVE HAND *Boutique* is smack in the middle
of Tendon Street, its unique second story a raised
middle finger to the rest of the businesses on the strip.
A classy one, wearing cream gloves with an amethyst
for a door. From down the block, you could stop in at
the second-hand clothing shop, buy a cheap
hamburger the next store over, and wipe your hands on
a thin, paper napkin before turning *High Five*'s silver
handle. Inside, any hand you pick up costs no less than
an arm and a leg.

Best made hands around! the staff will tell
you. *Ethically sourced! Available in all colours, and all
means all, guaranteed!*

The displays are arranged on clean, silver
surfaces in a curved glass case that runs the perimeter
of the store: an anaemic hand with an undershade of
violet; bold vermillion knuckles that shimmer in
sunlight; a stylish masc collection, with everything from
the *Strong Silent Type* to *Get 'er Done* models.

Delicate track lighting hangs from the vaulted
ceiling, illuminating two black and white chaise lounges

in the centre of the room. A staircase runs up the right wall to an open loft. The sign strung across the base of the railing reads *Staff Only*.

Amber stands behind a hunk of sparkling black rock that splits into thousands of finger-like protuberances supporting the silver countertop. She struggles with a roll of coins, the finger-length of solid gold shrink-wrapped in plastic resisting her efforts. Her fingernails are no match. Exacto-knife to the rescue.

As $25 fills the tray, the silver bell over the front door scatters notes across the store. Amber closes the register and smooths the front of her velvet blazer, a friendly smile already in place. Her third eye flicks up to study the customers.

A sharp old woman wearing a trench coat and a young adult in a roughed-up camo jacket wipe their boots on the welcome mat. Melting snow shines like glitter in their hair. The younger one is familiar. Plain face, thin lips. Straight blonde hair cut just past their chin.

Amber places them—last night at *Beauty Mark*. Marius had invited her and Cam for drinks after work. But there was someone else already at the booth, a client, maybe, or one of the higher-ups from *High Five*'s suppliers. There was something unsettling about him, though she couldn't put a finger on what it was. The blonde customer was alone at a table by the dance floor. The client whispered something to Marius. Handing something to Cam under the table, Marius had sent him over to deliver a crumpled paper bag. *Just a work thing*, Cam had deflected when she asked him about it later.

"Hello," Amber calls professionally to the two customers. "Can I give you a *hand* with anything?"

Trenchcoat and blondie approach her grimly. Not even a groan for her clever pun? Amber feels a twinge of disappointment.

Trenchcoat takes a paper bag from her pocket and sets it on the counter. "We'd like to make a return."

Amber recognizes the bag, the logo. "That's one of our samples."

"Is it in the best interest of this store to be giving out *children's fingers* as samples?"

"There must be a mistake." Her third eye blinks innocently.

"I don't think so," Trenchcoat growls, glancing down to read her name tag. "Amber. I'd like to speak with your manager."

"Of course, I'll see if he's available." She picks up the store handheld and holds down the "1" key to connect with the loft phone. "There are two customers here with a question about one of the samples."

"Thank you, Amber." Marius's voice is scratchy through the phone line. "I want to talk to them alone."

"I understand."

"Half an hour should be enough."

"I'll be in the back if you need me." Amber returns the handheld to its stand. "He'll be right down. Feel free to browse." Amber widens her smile and takes a box of unseparated price labels to the back room.

Earbuds in, Amber hums along to her playlist as her fingers tear each row of white stickers down each perforated line. When she emerges half an hour later, the store is empty. She picks up the handheld, her thumb hovering over the "1" key.

Replacing the phone in its cradle, she works her pinky fingernail between her two front teeth. Not biting it. Her hand is from Monday's new shipment and is too valuable to even think about biting. After all, it isn't really hers.

CHAPTER EIGHT
Crooked Teeth

IT'S THE SUNGLASSES guy from *Beauty Mark*. I mean, I shoulda known, right? The three-eyed brunette is here, so why not him too? The way he owns the store's curved staircase as he descends, that suave close-lipped smile, a form-fitting suit? Must be made of money, or so he wants everyone to think.

He steps easily over the *Staff Only* sign, and glides behind the counter. "I see you got my message."

"You knew how to get a hold of me," Jessica says evenly. "Why all the drama, why involve my friend?"

He shrugs, the bright store lights gleaming off his sunglasses. "The client asked me to deliver it the way it would have the most impact."

Jessica places her hands on either side of the paper bag.

"It's not for you anyway," Marius says. "It's for your reclusive ward." His grin is shocking, the rest of him so well put together and then his crooked teeth crowding forward in his mouth.

"How'd you know I'd deliver it?" I ask, legitimately curious. I mean, two days ago I had no idea Jessica Fit was a name, let alone a person.

His lips close over his teeth in a charming smile. "Find me at the *Beauty Mark* any Saturday night. I'll show you a good time."

The exit light in my head flickers, a slip of red in the dark.

"Marius," Jessica cuts him off.

"Only sweet, sweet Reena knows what this is about. That's all I can tell you." He points with a flat hand towards the door. "Don't let me *inconvenience* you further."

"I'm used to your threats. Don't think they'll have any more impact than they did five years ago."

"That long? Well, always nice to catch up."

Jessica is already halfway to the door. I trip over myself trying to catch up. Marius's shaded eyes drill into the back of my head like two sharpened fingernails.

We burst out into the street, icy air clawing through our clothes. I piece the ends of my coat zipper together; Jessica's trench coat flaps open, her face radiating something I haven't seen from her before. She rubs the corner of her mouth and strides up the sidewalk. It isn't far to her apartment, but I hurry after her anyway, afraid of being left behind.

I pull the hood of the camouflage jacket over my hair. "Thanks again for the coat," I say, finally reaching her.

The corner of her mouth rises slightly, but she says nothing.

We reach the base of the stairs leading up to her apartment. "I'm sorry about all of this. Don't worry. Marius won't bother you. He's only interested in people who will pay him."

"What do the fingers have to do with Reena anyway?" I ask, hoping to extend the conversation a little longer. Being around Jessica feels safe, stabilising. Last night has left me more shaken than I realised.

"I don't know." She notices me lingering. "You can come up if you want. My door's always open, Nan."

"Nah," I say, digging in the snow with my shoe. "It's getting late."

"Tomorrow, then."

"Cool," I nod.

Jessica mounts the stairs. She holds up her keys and raises her eyebrows. That time I ran after her trying to return her mouth. A joke between us now.

I wave and head further down Tendon Street. The shops give way to a government plaza with a grey-brown front lawn. A few blocks later, rows of low-income housing with open porches and fake cast iron fences around empty garden beds. Maybe I'll go to that coffee place on the riverfront, kill a few hours—

"Hey, Camouflage!" The call comes from a smoker perched on a bus bench. They're wearing a white blouse and a silk vest under an open felt coat. Their hair curls out from under a wide-brimmed fedora festooned with a bunch of dried wildflowers. "What's the time?" they ask, their mascaraed eyes crimped and intense, as if bringing something far away into focus.

"What?"

"The time, o'clock."

I dig my phone out of the coat's deep pocket and glance at the screen. "5:02."

"5:02, 5:02. Thanks."

"Anytime."

They exhale smoke, one hand propped up in their vest pocket. "Hey, Camouflage!" they yell after me. "Don't lose yourself out there!"

CHAPTER NINE
Narrow View

THE YEAR AFTER my parents got divorced, I didn't socialise much. Went to school and back, stayed in my room the rest of the time. Wasn't moping or anything. I just didn't feel like talking.

Mom, on the other hand, started going out; like she needed people to distract her, like my silences at home were painful. Most of the time, I didn't know or care where she went.

Our house had, still has, a wall-to-wall bookshelf in the living room. Mom studied literature on a scholarship before she dropped out to have me. I made good use of her collection that first, quiet year. Read a lot of classics, poetry, that kind of thing. And when she'd bang through the front door at two in the morning, pretty much shit-faced, I'd stuff my book under my pillow and pretend to be asleep.

But now, I'm the one coming home at 2 a.m. Sometimes she's still up, but usually the house is dark. Foreboding, that wall of bookshelves, sucking up light and keeping quiet. Like a great, gaping mouth I could fall into.

Tonight, there's a light in the kitchen.

"Hey Mom," I say, heading to the fridge. Orange juice, maybe? I pour a glass and return the jug to the top shelf. The fridge door seals behind me, hums.

Her attention stays fixed on her tablet. "Have a good day?" Looks like she's playing solitaire or something.

"Nothing special." That's when I notice. "You replaced it."

She looks up, surprised. "I said I would, didn't I?"

"It—it looks…"

"Yes, I agree. Much better."

She winks her new eye, the one that used to be blue with the pupil set far to the left. Growing up, her family was too poor to buy her a new one. Kids would make fun of her, call her "the lizard kid," shit like that. Even as an adult, she still got weird looks sometimes. But I liked it. It was like she could see slightly more than other people could, like her range of vision wasn't as narrow.

The new eye is pale green to match her other one and the pupil is dead centre.

I can't be upset. "Your face, I guess."

Her mouth folds into itself, leaving a hard line behind. Christ, now I've hurt her feelings. I scramble around for something to say. Instead, I drain the orange juice and set the empty glass on the counter.

"Put that away," she snaps.

The rest of the counter is spotless, the vinyl bleached clean. I open the dishwasher and overturn the glass, maneuvering it under the counter and onto the top rack.

"Happy now?" I head for the stairs.

She doesn't reply, both eyes intent on the game in front of her.

Sometimes, I wish she hadn't gotten her liver replaced, all that rehab. She was so much easier to talk to when she was drunk.

INTERLUDE TWO:
Jessica's Adam

ADAM VISITS HOME a few times a year. Usually in the winter, when the crowds come looking for coats. He'll stay a week or two, then head out again. There was one year he stayed almost until spring, but that was for reasons that had nothing to do with me.

Reena moved in with us when Adam was fifteen. Was that seven years ago already? A friend of mine who runs a retreat centre recommended her, and I invited her to stay with us.

She was sixteen then and impressively self-controlled. It was obvious to both Adam and myself that she had been through something terrible, but we never asked her about it. We were intrigued by her self-imposed periods of silence and fasting. She brought one small suitcase with her; inside were two loose-fitting grey dresses, a yellow hardback copy of the *Tao Te Ching* translated into English, and a cloth bag containing a bar of soap, a comb, and a pair of scissors. To this day, she keeps her curly black hair cut short.

She was far from demure, however. Quite forceful at times with her language. For a while, Adam would say anything to set her off. Not that he was trying to upset her. Reena enjoyed the challenge, and Adam finally had someone other than me to talk to.

"I think I may trade in my eyes today," he would start, setting his homework on the table where Reena was working through a library book on Daoism in North America.

"Alright," she would say, turning the page.

"Green is a much more *handsome* colour, don't you think?"

"They're not your eyes to keep anyway."

"But," Adam would grin, his colourless eyes glinting with mischief, "I'm buying new eyes because they look nice. Isn't that being vain?"

"It's like self-conducted reincarnation in a way. No, listen..."

And off they would go, for hours. And so it went, for a few golden years.

Adam finished high school. Around that time, he and Reena had a falling out over something rather serious. They never would tell me what it was about, though I can guess.

Adam decided to go travelling. Reena stayed here, studying, meditating, sewing up lost causes of coats. She could have taken an exam to get a high school diploma, but she didn't want to. I don't have the weight of parenthood to hold over her: I can only advise. At least, that's how I see it.

Adam returned the following winter and stayed with us for a week. He told us all about the places he'd been, the people he'd met. And then off he went again. It was the same the next year. But the year after that, that was the year he stayed.

"You've started wearing colours," he noted to Reena over breakfast.

Reena was wearing a red hoodie over her usual grey.

"I like—I mean, it's nice."

Reena's face flushed enough to match the sweater. "It was a gift. There's nothing to say I shouldn't accept the generosity of others, is there?"

Adam winked at me, in that easy way of his, but he fumbled a spoonful of sugar, the utensil dropping onto a saucer and cracking it all the way through.

"What's the matter?" I asked.

It turned out that he had a fever of 105.

CHAPTER TEN
Scab

A BLACK CAT sleeps on the chair with a missing slat, in the perfect spot where the winter sunlight washes in through the apartment's sliding patio door, almost warm. The cat curls in on himself, his eye a thin golden slit as he purrs and expands with breath and curls in again.

"What's his name?" I ask, crouching on the balls of my feet.

"No Name," Reena huffs from the entryway. She adds a newly-mended plaid coat to the rack, spacing the dozen or so coats further along the metal bar.

"No Name, like the chips." I tip my head a little, trying to match the cat's angle.

As if she hasn't heard—I know she has—Reena moves through the living room behind me. I keep my eyes on No Name, but I hear Reena shut her bedroom door, the handle latching closed. The whirr of a sewing machine buzzes through the wall.

"How is sleep, little cat? Do you feel safe here?"

No Name purrs and tucks his head further into the warm circle of his body.

I let my butt hit the ground and lean back until my shoulder blades meet the rug; the back of my head finds a comfortable spot. I stare at the textured ceiling. There's a greyish watermark bubbling out from over the patio door, but other than that, it's a pristine, eggshell white that reminds me of a full moon.

There's something about this place. Crossing one ankle over the other, I pick at a scab on the back of my left forearm and take a deep breath through my nose. It doesn't smell any better than my house. Worse, if I'm honest, like settled dust and shoe leather, leftover cooked chicken and something old and floral, like lavender left too long in a jar of water. But the smells are richer than the recycled air and sanitised kitchen Mom is so proud of. The smells here feel solid and real. They tell me that things are happening, and that I am part of them.

When I wake up, No Name is curled right next to my ear, his low purr reverberating through my skin. I sit up and he jogs down to my knee. Placing a paw on my leg, he effortlessly jumps onto my lap. No Name nudges my fingers until I give in and scratch behind his ears. Christ, I can't remember the last time I pet a cat.

The lock turns in the front door and No Name takes off, running around Jessica's feet and out onto the fire escape. She looks after him, then closes the door.

"You lost your cat," I say.

"Not my cat to lose," she replies, quirking an eyebrow at me. "Did you like him?"

"He's cute."

Jessica lowers a full reusable shopping bag to the floor and crouches down to untie her hiking boots. "He was so skittish when Reena first brought him home. He used to tear around the house, rip up anything he could get his claws into. But he's mellowed out over time. He still likes to go out, but he always comes back."

"Reena called him No Name."

"That's right." She frees one of her sock feet. "Do you have any pets?"

"Nah, my mom thinks they're too much trouble to be worth it."

"And the cat hair," Jessica empathises. "It's a constant struggle, but we struggle on."

"Is that what happened to all your furniture?"

"No Name? Oh no. We sold most of it last year." She removes the other boot and places the pair under the sparsely-populated coat rack.

My cheeks get warm, but I ask anyway. "Are you...y'know. Hard up for cash, or whatever?"

"Of course," she grins, brushing her white hair back from her forehead. "Does that make you uncomfortable?"

The warmth in my cheeks flares to a full flush. "Just, uh. You don't have to feed me, or, I don't have to come over..."

"Of course you're getting fed." She hands me the reusable bag with a serious gleam in her eyes. "But you're going to have to work for it."

Straining against the weight of the bag, I pull the handles open and peer inside. Jumbled at the bottom are a dozen brown potatoes and a bundle of grimy orange carrots.

"Finnnnnnnnne," I fake groan.

We laugh as I lug the bag to the kitchen sink.

Jessica hands me a peeler with a wooden handle and a lime green colander. "You get started on those. I'm going to see how Reena's doing."

Potatoes first. I gouge out the eyes, the pink-edged, white tubers sprouting through the tough skins. I cut away the scars and pits, wash each potato under the tap, turning them over in my hands, rubbing at the dirt with my palms. When they're clean, I place them in the colander until there's a mound of them rising above the green lip. I'm just peeling the first carrot, when Jessica comes up next to me.

"You're bleeding," she says, her sharp eyes catching the scab I picked open on my arm. "Band-aids are in the bathroom." She accepts the peeler and the carrot with a bright orange stripe.

I wipe my hands on my jeans, then meander my way around the three chairs in the dining area between the kitchen and the hallway. The bench from the other night is under a curtained window next to the counter, but there's no sign of the fold-up table.

Light from Reena's half-open door seeps into the dim hall. Something white and elegant stands in the middle of her room, with cloth leaves outlined in pale blue thread around the neckline. Reena is crouched at the hem, her back towards me. I stop for a moment, surprised that she's working on what could only be a wedding dress. She turns, her lips pursed, a row of pins bristling between them.

I quickly move through the dim hall, feeling more than seeing my way to the bathroom. Daylight spills in through a frosted window above the bathtub, overflowing onto the paisley linoleum and splashing up the pale blue walls. I close the door and press the button in the handle to lock it.

Bathrooms and me, we have a good relationship: as long as I wash my hands on the way out, I can stay as long as I like. I take my time, sitting on the plush mat draped over the side of the tub, considering the juvenile watercolour painting of a sailboat above the toilet.

Deep in that dark place, I imagine the connection between my left forearm and my elbow. I have to focus—it's always been harder for me to detach my arms and hands. Taking a breath, I ease the part away, let it go until my elbow joint tingles painfully.

Trying not to jostle my thoughts too much, I pull my left forearm free and set it across my knees, the still-attached hand brushing my shin. I locate the oozing wound. The scab hangs on by a thread of skin. I pinch the scab free and wrap it in a piece of toilet paper. Dab the blood away.

Carrying my arm to the stand-alone sink, I press my abdomen tight to the ceramic to keep the part from rolling off. I catch a glimpse of myself in the mirror, look away. A distant hum buzzes through my right hand. Falls silent.

Inside the mirror cabinet are band-aids, along with a shaving kit in a leather case, a white bottle of painkillers, and a half-flattened tube of toothpaste. There's also a spray bottle of hydrogen peroxide, which I move down into the sink. I manage to single-handedly free a band-aid from the box.

Taking the hydrogen peroxide, I spray the still oozing cut, wipe away the bubbling foam. I rip the paper packaging from the band-aid with my teeth. My fingers butterfly the flaps open. I match the sterile pad to the cut, pressing the adhesive wings to my skin. The crisp plastic tabs, packaging, and folded toilet paper flutter into the wire wastebasket.

Curling my fingers around the wrist, I pick up the disembodied arm. I take a deep breath. In one motion, I swing the arm down and up so it lines up perfectly with my vacant left elbow. A thrill of satisfaction as the forearm *shhhhks* into place.

The tingling in my elbow fades into relief. And then the sting hits, sharp under the band-aid. I clench my left hand and spread out the fingers. I bend my arm at the elbow to check the back of my forearm. Success.

I wash my hands and leave the bathroom.

Reena's door is closed when I pass by. I wonder who the wedding dress is for, but I don't ask when Jessica says, "did you find everything okay?"

Instead, we finish making dinner. Reena joins us to eat at the counter—bowls of roasted vegetables and almonds on a bed of leftover quinoa.

Thirsty, I drop down from the barstool and round the counter into the kitchen proper. "Where's Adam?" I ask as casually as I can.

Reena's glare turns on me. "Why do you care?"

"He's catching up with some friends." Jessica sets down her fork. "He'll be back."

"Not that you'll be here," Reena pours on.

I'm relishing what I'm about to say next, directed at Reena's squinty blue eyes. "You're the one who knows what those fingers are about. That Marius guy said."

Her posture deflates a bit. "I don't know what they mean."

"Well," Jessica grimaces. "I hate to ask this, Reena. I know you don't like to talk about it, but if these fingers are actually from a child…Is there any reason you can think of? Something from your past? Anyone who would—"

Reena straightens, her spine a rod, her body filling like a curtain in the wind. "No." She shakes her head at Jessica. "No," she says again. She disembarks, storms towards the entryway.

The front door slams and the fire escape stairs bang. There is only her angry absence.

"Someone's got problems," I say, taking a carton of milk from the fridge.

"Don't we all?" Jessica passes me a glass. "Let's see what we can find out."

CHAPTER ELEVEN
Third Eye

AMBER'S FINGERS RUN through 5s, 10s, 20s, 50s, and 100s. She seals the stack in a plastic bag, writes the date on the dotted line. Her fingertips press the digital combination for the safe under the till. Taking out a white plastic case with rounded corners, Amber sets it on the counter and pops off the lid, revealing the two hands resting inside.

Right hand removes the left hand from her wrist and replaces it with the left hand from the case. She uses her left hand to switch out the right hand. The two removed hands, the ones she's been working with all day, fit perfectly into the foam inserts. She seals them inside the case, placing the money bag on top before lowering them into the safe. She waits for the final click of the mechanism to lock the door in place.

Marius left two hours ago, muttering into his embedded earphone. She doesn't have enough money for tech-parts, not yet. She's hoping to buy her work-model hands in a few months, once she's saved up.

Cameron's already given her trouble over the third eye she bought herself for Christmas.

Whatever.

Coat, keys, cell phone, and purse from the back room.

Lights out.

One last look around and she can call it a night.

Amber's third eye roves over the dark display cases. The streetlight glare glows on the just-swept floor. A couple of figures pass outside the shop front, stopping briefly to peer into the dim interior.

We're closed, obviously! Amber thinks at them. She's relieved when they leave without banging on the window.

Maybe she should check upstairs.

One light back on, bringing the staircase out of the shadows. She reads a text message from Cameron as she ascends to the loft: *meet u @ BM??*

Yeah, she types back, *just closing up.*

There's enough light bleeding from the single track light for her to recognize the shape of the loft's desk, closet, and filing cabinet. There's another safe up here, too, for special deliveries and paperwork. A small office loft with limited legroom and nothing out of the ordinary.

She's about to descend when she notices the gleam on the desk. A glass cup or jar that Marius forgot to take down to the break room. She picks it up. Some leftover liquid swashes against the inside.

As she makes her way back towards the stairs, the light fills the jar and illuminates the contents: blue liquid, like window cleaner, with something suspended in it, tubular and fleshy like a thickset worm. She holds it up, her third eye clenched in horror.

Floating in the jar is a child's finger, its purple nail polish catching the light.

CHAPTER TWELVE
Middle

Winter wind pummels my back, disturbs the snowdrifts huddling in the evening shadows of Tendon Street. The road and the sidewalks bristle with cracks, damp spots of melted ice and salt scattered across. I work the collar of my camo coat up to my nose, breathing out into the material, trying to warm it.

"What are we looking for?" I ask Jessica. Not much to go on: Marius, a paper bag, sparkly fingernails.

"Someone who might have more answers than we do."

We stop outside of *High Five*. The lights are off, but I can make out a figure behind the desk. The sign hanging over the window display has been flipped over to read *Closed*.

"Over here." Jessica points down the alley between *High Five* and the burger joint.

Following, I skirt around the grey plastic bins puking up bags of fast food trash. A hooded fluorescent light glares down over the boutique's side exit.

"Keep an eye out," Jessica whispers. She sits on her heels with her back against the burger joint wall. I crouch next to her, the grey metal door in my sightline. I clench my hands into fists and cram them in my pockets.

The wind picks up in bursts that rush through the alley. A fine mist of snow condenses on the side of my face. I pass my cheek over my shoulder, wipe the cold dampness away.

After a few long minutes, the door pushes open, casting a long shadow that points directly towards us.

Jessica waits until the three-eyed clerk locks the door. As Amber returns the key to her coat pocket, Jessica launches from behind the garbage bin looking every bit like a hawk diving at its prey.

"Don't hurt me!" Amber yells, backing against the door and fumbling for something in her purse.

Jessica stops mid-stride, her posture sharp and her face grim. "You recognize us?"

Amber nods, her third eye flicking across to me.

"Do you know what was in the paper bag I showed you?"

Her angled haircut comes apart at the seams as she shakes her head.

"A child's finger."

The clerk's three eyes widen.

"Do you know anything about that?"

"I..." She shivers, pulling her caramel coat close around her. "There was another one. In Marius's office."

"Who's supplying them?"

"How the hell should I know?"

Jessica's frown deepens. "I don't believe you. You're part of it, you work for him—"

Amber's hand reaches into her purse. "Marius doesn't tell me shit." She frees a pen-sized white case. "I was going to ask Cam about it, but…if you want to take this, be my guest."

"Thank you," Jessica says, but doesn't relax. "You might want to reconsider working here."

Amber's third eye narrows. "This didn't happen."

"You can arrange it to look like whatever you want. Marius will know I was here." Done with the clerk, Jessica strides out of the alley, and waits for me on the sidewalk.

"Another one?" I ask as I reach her.

Jessica only grips the white case.

CHAPTER THIRTEEN
Fever

"ADAM HAD A fever of 105."

"What was it?" I ask, hoping Jessica will continue the story. Anything to break the monotony of unloading box after box of refurbished boots onto the shoe rack.

"A virus, maybe."

"Did you take him to the hospital?"

"Initially. They gave him antibiotics and told us to keep him warm and hydrated."

"But he was really sick, right?"

"The new healthcare guidelines meant that Adam no longer had medical coverage for extended hospital stays; he was unemployed, out of school, and too old to be considered a dependent. The doctor advised us to take him home."

"How...how sick was he?"

Jessica sets a pair of hiking boots on the rack. "He could have died."

"But he didn't."

"He didn't. We wrapped him in blankets, put a cup of water and a pill bottle on the nightstand, and hoped. Reena set up a chair next to the bed. She stayed there for three days. After that, she would visit his room regularly to read to him, or tell him things she had done or seen or thought about during the day. But as he grew healthier, she stayed less and less."

Jessica stares into the almost empty box. "Adam took another month to fully recover. He was thinner than usual, if you can imagine that, and drained. If he was feeling up to it, he'd help wash dishes, or sweep the floor. When Reena got home from the library or after visiting the meditation centre, his face would positively light up. They'd talk at the table for hours."

Something tugs at me—a familiarity, a knowledge that I can't quite accept. Adam and Reena's accidental touch at the dinner table, the way his voice changed when he complimented her. Did he have feelings for Reena? The idea strikes deep, a cut to the heart.

Jessica unloads the last pair of shoes and slowly breaks down the cardboard box. "Around that time, I got a phone call from a friend in the county. Their partner had left drunk and angry, and they were afraid to spend the night alone in their little farmhouse. So I hitched a ride with a mutual friend, telling Reena I'd be back late the next day. When I got home, Adam was gone."

"Where? Why?" I ask, wondering if I really want to know.

"Adam asked something, I think. And Reena said no." Jessica sighs. "It's never been the same between them since."

CHAPTER FOURTEEN
Headspace

SHE SITS AT the bar in the *Beauty Mark*, but the club is empty. The wide velvet booths sag in relief; the dance floor takes a smoke break.

"What'll it be, doll?" The bartender smiles knowingly. They have a wide alabaster forehead, their arched eyebrows are drawn on.

She says something to them.

"You can't drink that here," their left nostril raises in disgust. "What about a gin martini instead?"

A tapered glass appears in front of her. Rolling in the clear liquid is an eyeball. She picks up the glass and swirls the alcohol, drinks it slowly.

"Well, well, well." The sunglassed man sidles up next to her. "Never thought you'd actually come. Didn't Jessica warn you not to get involved with me? According to her I'm," he casually readjusts his sunglasses, "bad goods."

She keeps drinking, though she's noticed the delicate hand gripping her thigh.

"A toast for the occasion," he says. He raises the drink in his other hand, a smoking blue concoction that she can't name. "I think you're a pretty special girl. Not my usual type, but I can make some changes. Would you like that? A smaller chin, a cuter hairline, a couple of tweaks here and there. You could be really gorgeous, a knock out." Crowded teeth peer through his lips.

Her drink has mysteriously been refilled. She drains it and lowers the glass onto the bartop. The hollow click of glass on marble opens up the room and thousands of faceless people rush in.

"She's ready." Marius nods to the bouncer.

Iron hands clench around her arms. A rope tightens across her chest. The bouncer's bullet eyes pin her to a reclining chair.

Marius appears in front of her. He shakes out his hands and places his palms on her temples. "This will only hurt a little."

A seam opens across her neck. A scream tears out of it and is cut off.

"There," Marius says. "Just one more—"

The bouncer stands between her and her body, busy with something. Her body. She clearly sees it, the bulky shoulders, the flat chest, the awkward hips.

"Remember…" A tenor voice croons in her ear, the words spinning through her decapitated head. "Reena…in the side…in the side…"

Suddenly, she is the one in the chair—she has lost sight of herself—

"Beautiful," Marius appraises.

The bouncer holds up a mirror. She knows that the reflected image is her. But the face is not hers, the hair is not hers, the hand is not hers—

"Christ!" she moans, and tries to run, but Marius's fingers clamp onto her temples, pressing his face against her forehead.

"Stop it! Get the fuck away! Stop!"

I push back against the weight, throwing it off me. For a while, there's only breathing. Is it mine?

It's dark. It was never full of people. I'm home. This is my bed, my room. I pull my comforter back towards me. My temples throb. I remember drinking three beers before bed and I feel nauseous. Mom went out. I was home alone. I took a half-empty six pack out of the fridge and drank the rest, one after the other.

My heartbeat pounds against my chest. Tumbling through formless thoughts, no sense of time. Just a long night ahead and no desire to re-enter my dreams. My eyelids flip open. The slightest hum of the basement furnace startles me awake.

I turn on the lamp. After a moment, I tip the base up from the nightstand. Underneath is a flat metal key. And something else.

Sitting up, I peel the rectangle from the bottom of the round base. It's a Polaroid, the edges tinged blue by light leak. I hold it under the lampshade for a better look. A summer park. A figure in the centre, laughing. Blue hair, tanned skin, wearing a t-shirt and cut-off shorts. One hand holds a tree branch covered in flowers, the other rests easy on their hip. Do I…know them?

The remnant of my nightmare rears over me. Another mystery on top of everything else is too much. I return the Polaroid to its hiding place.

There's a drawer in the nightstand. I unlock it with the flat metal key. Inside is a white case with rounded edges. I open it so that the lid rests next to it in the drawer. Then, I take out my eyes. The right eye. The left eye.

It's darker still, the most impenetrable dark. I hold my eyes gently in one hand, feel for the lid in the drawer. Placing my eyes in the box, I nick my hand on the wooden edge of the table. My nervous fingers find the eyes, still sitting comfortably in the box. I place the lid on top, feel for the corners with both hands, secure it. The drawer rattles closed. I lock it and replace the key under the lamp and the Polaroid.

I'm still awake. But now the dark is total, and after a moment of panic, my brain begins to slow down. Not much I can do in the dark. Only wait.

CHAPTER FIFTEEN
Unmentionables

MY PLACE IN *10.*

Amber reads the text again. The tone's cramped, short on patience. Either Cam's in the middle of a job, or he's desperate. She smiles a little. It's been a few days since they've been together and she's hungry herself.

She stands in the middle of her bedroom, trying to decide if it's worth it. If it's going to be rushed, there's no point. He won't notice anyway. But if it's going to be an all-night affair, that's a different story. She'll dress up.

"What the hell," she decides, reaching an arm through her hanging blouses to a shelf at the back of her closet. Her fingers catch on the smooth case. She opens it on her bed and loses her skinny jeans, her thong. Removing her vulva, she fits the piece from the box between her legs.

"Mmm," she relaxes. Even after a year, her party vag is still something else. Not as comfortable as her original, but it'll make for an exciting night.

She places her original inside the box, seals it, and returns it to its hiding place.

Amber buttons up a pair of fancy, high-waisted, denim jeans, chooses a semi-see-through cream blouse. She touches up the eyeliner on her third eye, smiles at herself.

Be right there, she texts.

#

Amber knocks again, banging a little louder with the outside of her fist. She takes her phone from her purse, but before she can type a message, the door swings open.

"Did you forget I was coming?" she calls into the apartment. All the lights are off, except for a faint glow radiating from around the kitchen wall. "Cameron?"

She closes the door quietly, gripping the phone in her hand. The glow draws her through the living room, around the corner, into the breakfast nook.

Marius and Cameron sit at the table, a brown paper bag between them. Marius is drinking a beer, and even though there's a bottle in front of Cam, it's clear he hasn't touched it.

"What the hell is this?"

Marius's hand pauses, the bottle mouth inches away from his, which creeps up into a grin.

"Need your help on this one, babe," Cameron says without looking at her.

"The catered event isn't until tomorrow. You already set up the tables at the *High Five*, didn't you? What do you need me for?"

"This is a special case," Marius says casually. He takes a final sip. "Tell her, Cam."

Cameron's hand teases the beer in front of him, his pupils fixated on the label. "There's a delivery."

Marius slides his chair back and stands, holding his empty bottle loosely in his hand. His walk is so smooth he seems to ooze around the counter between the nook and the kitchen. A set of novelty wings arch from the back of his suit jacket, spanning shoulder to shoulder. Black and white feathers with velvet red tips. Specially developed to hook into the wearer's shoulder muscles. More than she could ever afford.

"What do you want me to do about it?" she asks, her irritation starting to give way to a tight feeling in her throat.

Marius places the bottle next to the sink. He turns around to face her, as serious as she's ever seen him. "I know you gave Jessica Fit that finger." The wings flair up from behind him and settle back out of sight.

Amber shivers and passes it off with a shrug. "So what if I did? You were going to deliver it anyway."

"Our client had a very specific schedule in mind. Breaching that contract is not something I want to have on my conscience."

"So we're dealing in underage parts now?" Amber cuts in despite the knot pressing against the inside of her abdomen. Something about Marius is off. He's serious, using his wings to impress her, remind her who's in charge. But there's a faint tic at the corner of his mouth, pulling downwards. He doesn't let it move more than a centimetre. Amber imagines what would happen if he let go: the tic would pull all the way down to the floor, rip his face open.

"We're delivering them. That's all. After this, no more kid stuff. We'll be back to the way it was, ethically sourced, adult-only guaranteed. I promise."

That's when it hits her. What's off about Marius—he's afraid of something.

He leans on the counter, shadows filling his cheeks. "I can also promise that if you do this right, there will be…opportunities for you to advance in this business."

Amber's stomach flips, excitement replacing her dread. Advancement? Like, a promotion? No more counting the deposit, no more sweeping floors?

"You said you needed my help?" she turns to Cam, who's slunk down in his chair. "Cameron!"

"Yeah." He finally meets her eyes. "I said you would."

"It's the fourth finger," Marius nods to the paper bag. "I'm supposed to deliver it directly."

"And?" Amber presses him.

"And she's gone."

"Who?"

"Reena."

"Who the hell is Reena?"

But Marius doesn't answer. His eyes wander as he sinks back into the chair next to Cam. "It's not for certain, but *he* said—" Marius pulls Cam's beer bottle towards him, takes a commanding sip. "There's a retreat centre." He reaches a hand across the table and grips Amber tightly by the wrist. "And only you can go there."

CHAPTER SIXTEEN
Two-Faced

"I HEARD YOU coming up the stairs. Come on in!"

I close the apartment door behind me, take the mug Jessica offers. She seems vulnerable, this early in the morning, in a grey, cable-knit sweater and black sweatpants.

Coffee in hand, we sit on the two folding chairs facing the patio door. She stretches her bare feet out on the rug. One of her toes sticks out, distinguished by a square nail bed. Not an original piece, based on the rounded nails on her other nine toes.

"You're married?" I ask, recognizing the traded digit as a common wedding tradition.

She studies the toe for a moment, her angled profile softening into the past. Before I can ask anything further, she's sharp again. "I took the middle finger we got from Amber to the hospital. They're going to keep all of the fingers on file, in case someone claims them."

We sip in silence, looking out at the dreary city framed by the patio door. Beyond Tendon Street rises the jagged jaw of downtown, buildings curving up like sharp teeth. I don't ask where Reena or Adam are. Seems like they've been dealing with their own shit lately. Besides, any room without Reena in it is fine by me.

"I've been meaning to ask you," I say instead. "Why'd you take off your mouth? The day we met, I mean. You had it crunched up in a napkin. Left it there."

Her mouth curls down at the corners. "I was upset."

"What about?"

"I was walking through the mall, and I saw a poster. It was gaudy, some kind of Ear-Tech sale. But there was a child in the picture. And that pissed me right off!" She inhales sharply through her nose. "These companies, trying to sell products to kids before they even know what the products are really for!"

"The kids don't get it though. They're too young, right? Goes over their heads."

"I still don't like it." Jessica grimaces.

"When was your first time?"

"Oh, I was 10." Jessica releases a breath, and I feel like I've defused a bomb. "A bit of an early bloomer. You'll never guess."

"Your mouth."

Jessica nodded. "After swimming class. I was in the locker room, laughing with the other kids, and then suddenly, I wasn't. Luckily, I found my mouth on the floor before anyone stepped on it."

"You were a swimmer?" I say quickly, before she can return the question.

"My parents wanted me to be prepared in case of a shipwreck. I'm not joking. We had to take a ferry whenever we visited my grandparents. They wanted to eliminate as much danger as was possible." Jessica sighs, almost sad. "Do you live with your parents?"

"Just my mom. Why?"

Jessica weighs my answer. "Don't take this the wrong way. I helped run a youth centre some years ago and I met a lot of street kids. You remind me of them. A wariness, a submerged, fierce strength. Well, not so submerged sometimes," she chuckles.

A pang of panic hits me, echoing deep through my insides. The nightmare breaks over me like a sour wave—my body is strapped in the chair—the face in the mirror that isn't mine—

"You're always welcome here," Jessica continues. "I've really appreciated your help."

Suddenly, my right hand grips the coffee mug too tight, spilling half of the drink on the rug. The fingernails dig into the painted porcelain. It wants to hurt someone, it wants to break—

Stop! I want to yell, but something prevents me. The hand smashes the mug on the floor and strains across the gap, fingers screaming for violence, clawing towards Jessica's neck—

My legs are still my own. I sprint for the kitchen. The hand latches onto the counter, fingers bending as they press into the stainless steel sink. I try to shake it loose, gripping my wrist with my free hand. It won't let go, it won't stop, it's going to break into pieces—

"Nan? What's happening?" Jessica warily follows me into the kitchen. Her eyes narrow, as if this is something she's seen before.

"I can't help it!" The hand contorts into a fist.

"Have you replaced it lately?"

I shake my head.

"You're lying."

"I've never replaced anything! Not even when I broke my collarbone. I let it heal! I swear to Christ!"

Her talon-like grip reaches for the hand, nails digging into my wrist.

"Stop!"

The hand goes limp. From under the skin, a blue icon rises to the surface.

Jessica's expression screws into a dozen iterations between grief and fury. She releases my wrist and walks over to the art wall.

I hold up my now limp appendage. The icon is a hand inside of a ring. Same as on the paper bag. It's a product stamp. The synthetic part's been reset to factory settings, under nobody's control now. Limp and fuzzy. I can't feel the fingers.

"Jessica," I follow her, a sick feeling in my gut, "I swear—"

"Why! T-tell me why?" She struggles with the words, too many of them trying to get out at once. "You didn't just find my mouth in the bathroom, did you? You were already following me. You were supposed to—supposed to find a way to gain my trust and wait for the right moment. Is that right? Fff—Fu—" Her lips press together. Her nostrils flare and her sharp eyes gleam along the edges. "I don't know who you are or why you're working for Marius, and I don't care." She takes a step closer. "Get out."

Words are suddenly burning things, scalding my throat. I need to vomit. I almost hope she'll run after me as I bash my way out the front door.

The stairwell railing bars my chest. My mouth tangles and saliva runs out of it in strings. Nothing else comes up.

The lock behind me scrapes shut.

Time passes. My body calms until I can take a breath without feeling sick. I cut the connection and remove the *High Five* hand from my right wrist.

It's time to go.

CHAPTER SEVENTEEN
Do Up Your Face

AMBER STEPS DOWN from the van. Her nose crinkles as a loose clump of snow tumbles into the mouth of her low-cut hiking boot. Sharp alpine air picks at her knitted sweater and black leggings, lifts the fringe of hair sticking out along the edge of her toque, purchased at the last gas station. It's scratchy and grey and probably makes her look cheap and down on her luck, but that's what Marius wants. The worn-out sweater and the bruised cheekbones that he insisted she wear, they're all calculated. Her unfamiliar hand grips the handle of a battered blue duffel bag.

As the van pulls away, she takes a few steps towards the rustic building. Two tree-trunk pillars support a permanent awning, heaped with snow. The recently-salted walkway beneath it leads to a set of varnished wooden doors, a surveillance camera built into its generous frame. Amber stops and turns slightly, watching as the van disappears behind a row of lodgepole pines. The sound of the motor gradually fades, leaving her alone in front of Spring Waters Retreat Centre.

The entryway is guarded by a broad-shouldered guard who compares her ID card to a list on their cell phone. They return her fake ID and hold the door open for her. Warm air rushes past as she enters the foyer. Straight ahead is a fireplace framed by two sensible armchairs. To her left, a wooden desk. The person behind it is wearing a loose sweater and reading a paperback. A comfy turquoise scarf encircles their neck. Her red hair is pulled up into a messy bun.

"Oh, hello," they notice her and set the book aside. "Are you Deb?"

Amber nods, looking around the room.

"Where's your coat?" they ask, standing up from the desk and motioning to the armchairs in one graceful motion. "You must be freezing."

"I'm fine," Amber replies, but eagerly accepts the invitation.

"Can I get you anything? A cup of tea maybe?" She studies Amber's face. They have blue-green eyes, bright and piercing. Amber suspects they're gauging her against the other visitors who come here, trying to figure out what she needs.

"I t-t-" Amber forces the stutter. "I talked to you on the phone."

"Yes, you're all set. You can stay for as long as you want." They sit down in the other armchair.

"It's safe, right? My friend, she said, she said that I'll be safe here."

"That's right," they reply, noting the way Amber's hands twist the handle of the duffel bag resting on her lap. "No one will bother you."

"I...I left my partner."

They nod, deciding what Deb needs. "We have his information on file. Even if he finds out where you are, he won't be able to get past the front door. You're safe here," they confirm. "My name's Carey. If you need anything while you're here, if you need anyone to talk to, just let me know."

Amber wipes an imaginary tear away with her borrowed hand. "Th-thank you."

"Why don't I bring you a cup of tea? You can stay here and warm up while I finish getting your room ready."

"Okay." Amber relaxes her hands, letting a hint of a smile creep over her mouth.

"I'll be right back." Carey gently gets up and smooths down the front of their sweater and jeans.

Amber waits until Carey's footsteps fade down the hallway. Then, she makes her way behind the desk, keeping one eye on the hall. She misses her third eye. In spite of the devastating headaches the first few days after the hospital installed it and the compatible forehead—the third eye, a synthetically-grown part, hooks into her left optic nerve, and the added strain took some getting used to—and a couple of discouraging comments from Cam, she'd grown to depend on it. She could search twice as fast if Marius allowed her to keep it on for this job. But he didn't want anything that Reena might recognize, although Amber is positive she's never seen Reena before in her life.

Under Carey's tattered science fiction novel is a leather-bound guest book. Amber turns to the page marked with a red ribbon. It lists the rooms currently occupied, with cleaning schedules pencilled in underneath. No names. She scans the entries from a week ago: a group of four rooms was cleaned last Monday, and a single bedroom was made up mid-week, when Reena is supposed to have arrived. *Room 22.*

Amber closes the book, resets the fanned-open paperback, and returns to the armchair.

Carey re-enters with a tray of tea things. She's accompanied by a middle-aged person dressed in grey and green loungewear under a long brown sweater. Xe wears a double chin, a bold forehead, and a collection of crow's feet that radiate around xyr acorn-brown eyes. Streaks of grey curl through xyr shoulder-length black hair.

Carey lowers the tray onto the round table between the two armchairs. "Deb, this is Lin. Xe runs the retreat centre."

"Welcome," Lin says, extending a hand.

Amber matches it briefly with her own, wondering if Deb should smile.

Lin watches her with a different expression from Carey. Less trying to find out what she needs and more trying to figure out who she is. "I hope your stay here will be helpful."

"I'm sure it will." Amber plays up a nervous half-smile to show that Deb is only being polite and is, in fact, still scared shitless.

"Carey will show you the way to your room when you're ready. We don't have many luxuries here, but if you need anything, please ask." Lin's crow's feet deepen. "Now, I should warn you. Our retreat centre draws people from many different faiths, many walks of life. We have a group here who are spending the week in silence, so don't feel offended if they don't start up a conversation."

"Okay."

"Dinner is at six o'clock, if you'd like to join us? I believe jambalaya is on the menu, but our cook has promised me nothing too spicy. Am I missing anything?" Lin turns to Carey.

Carey hands Amber a clay mug of tea. "I think you covered it all."

"Wonderful to meet you." Lin smiles at Amber, but it seems that there's something else in the smile, some small warning.

Amber-Deb brushes a stray hair from her purpled cheekbone. Lin's eyes flick to it, and the warning melts away. Amber silently thanks Marius for the borrowed part.

Room 22, Amber thinks to herself as Deb takes a timid sip of tea.

CHAPTER EIGHTEEN
Second Hand

JUST INSIDE THE doorway, the smell of incense fills my nose. Multicoloured curtains with mirrors sewn into the fabric cover the walls above the shelves and locked glass cabinets. The door brushes a set of wooden wind chimes as it rushes shut, like its only goal in life is to keep the smell of incense local to this seedy second-hand shop. The place is even called *Second Hand*, for Christ's sake.

"Feel free to look around," invites a voice from behind a tasselled curtain: the owner, I assume.

I don't remember ever doing this, looking for a new part. I don't remember my hand being switched. But it has a factory imprint. I wasn't born with it. I try to remember the last time I was blackout drunk, if someone could've taken it, switched it out for their own angry piece of flesh. Imagining it stirs a sick feeling in my stomach. I wander through the cases, holding the disembodied hand.

"Find anything you like?" The owner appears behind the long counter, framed by a cash machine and an upright leg dressed in neon-green fishnet and ankle bangles. They have long blond hair, bright green eyes, and a triangle chin, grown over with a day's worth of stubble.

"I want to trade-in," I say, walking up to them. "Do you do that here?"

"Oh, absolutely," the owner says, holding out an elegant hand. Their fingernails gleam the same green as the fishnets. "What you got?"

I hand over the hand, happy to be rid of it.

The owner whistles, turning it over and pulling each of the fingers. They press into the skin, like Jessica did. The blue *High Five* logo glows dimly. "This is really yours?"

I hold up my right arm, hoping the vacant wrist is enough to convince them I'm not lying. I didn't steal the thing. At least, I don't think I did.

The owner places the hand in a matte grey tray and presses a button. It's a bio scanner, a much smaller version of the ones hospitals use. They read the angled screen below the counter. "No infections or breaks. Almost new."

The owner removes their right hand and replaces it with my old one. "Very nice." They touch the thumb to each finger, grip the hand into a tight fist. "Are you sure you want to give this up?" My hand on their arm waves its fingers.

"Yes."

"Well," the owner says, removing my hand and re-attaching their own, "I can provide a replacement, no cost. This really is a gorgeous piece."

"Anything similar to that is fine."

The owner nods slowly, their green eyes preoccupied. "Why are you trading it in, I wonder..."

"Doesn't suit me anymore," I answer late, but the owner is already crouched down behind the counter.

They place three copper boxes with rounded corners in front of me. "These models are comparable. Try them on if you like. I'll give you a bit of privacy." Moving from behind the scanner, the owner flips back a square segment of the counter to create a door. As they pass through the narrow gap, their skirt catches on the underside of the countertop.

"Thanks," they smile as I single-handedly work the material free. Taking a tray of fingers over to one of the cabinets, they leave me alone as I open the three copper boxes.

The hand in the first case is tan, with thick knuckles and rounded nailbeds. A worker's hand, well-taken care of but rough.

The next hand is beige, with a double-jointed thumb and square nail beds. Younger than the other hand, maybe from a university student or an administrator, judging by the tell-tale callus on the side of the middle finger.

The third option is ruddy, fair hair on the back of it, with noticeable tendons and sharp knuckles. An athlete's hand.

I pick up the second box, thinking that the matching nail beds make it the best fit. But I'm drawn to the first hand. It seems more familiar, less threatening than the second one. Like I'll only disappoint the second hand, that I won't live up to its callus.

The first hand fits like a glove. I roll the wrist joint, curl the fingers. I look back at the owner—they're up on a step ladder, taking down a leg-length copper box from the top shelf.

Turning back to the counter, I go through the same thoughts as before: Jessica asking about my parents, how I remind her of street kids, the dream I had about Marius replacing my brain. The same panic, the same desire to vomit. But the new hand stays normal. In my control. No impulse to kill.

"I think I'm ready," I call, taking a moment to disconnect from the hand and place it back in the box.

"Wonderful!" the owner sings, hurrying over. Their skirt swings safely through the gap in the counter this time. "The first one, am I right?"

"Yes."

"Would you like to wear it out?" they ask, returning the two rejected hands under the counter. "And I can offer you an accessory or two, since the hand you brought in is in better condition. Any interest in our eyelid display—?"

"I was wondering."

"Yes? Don't be shy. Something else you're thinking?"

I attach the new hand to my arm, working out the stiffness in the fingers. My throat is suddenly tense. "Could you check something for me?"

"Of course. Thinking of making another trade?"

"I...I think that I may have been...tampered with."

They hesitate. "What kind of tampering?"

"Has anyone...ever brought in a brain before? I mean, maybe that's not even possible. Can you..." I point at the bio scanner tray.

The owner passes a hand along their stubbled cheek, frowning. "That one's only a retail model. Enough to check removed parts, but something like that?" Their green eyes reach steadily into mine. "You'll have to come in the back." They motion me towards the tasselled curtain.

This is a mistake. I'm probably freaking out over nothing. But that synthetic hand tried to kill Jessica. And that's something I would never do.

The back room is cramped. Open cupboards section the upper parts of the walls while two cluttered counters line either side underneath. A central workbench holds a tray of toes and a set of goose-styled wings half-wrapped in floral paper. Reams of colourful cloth spill out from rolls mounted to the walls. It has the feel of an old hat shop, with body parts and feathered accents on hand, ready to be added to new displays.

The owner leads me through to where two mauve armchairs sit on a braided rug. Between them is a polished wooden table, set with an antique chandelier lamp and a stick of incense angled in its holder.

We both sit, wordlessly. I rub my palms on my jeans.

"What do you remember?" the owner asks, lighting a match and holding it to the end of incense.

"I was talking with someone and my hand just— it tried to kill her. I could barely hold it back."

Smoke curls, wavering as the owner blows out the flame. The smell of a juniper forest fills the air.

"Anything else?"

"A dream I had." My eyelids blink and break through the memory. "They held me down. Talked about changing things. They…opened my head, did something…"

"Go ahead. It's alright."

"Please, just tell me if I'm crazy, or if you can fix it, I don't know—I don't know who I am, I could be anyone!"

They nod, frowning. "Do you want to be awake for it?"

"Yes," I manage.

Standing up, they straighten their green skirt. "If it hurts, tell me right away."

I take a deep breath, drawing incense into my nose.

"Try to relax."

Finding the dark place, I let go, let go, let go...

The owner peels off my forehead and opens my skull. "What the fuck is that?" they say, reaching in—

"Don't."

They lower their hands.

"Tell me."

The owner grimaces, tucking a loose piece of hair behind their ear. "There's something in there. A machine. Did you know?"

"Can you take it out?"

They shake their head. "I've had people come in with problematic parts before, but nothing...This is some messed-up shit."

After a moment, they replace my forehead. "Sorry. You could try the hospital, but they'd probably bring in the cops since there's brain tampering involved." Their green eyes carry a warning.

"Thanks."

They lead me out of the back room, around the counter, and halfway to the door. They pause next to a cabinet of ears. "Take care, okay?"

The chimes clatter overhead as I leave the store.

Cold startles me into awareness. A ringing crescendos in my ears. The front of my head aches with the knowledge of what's inside.

Out of the corner of my eye, I notice a group in long, wool coats coming down the sidewalk. They speed toward me, dress shoes grinding on the salted concrete. I've seen these people before, been restrained in their iron grips. A sharp pain cuts through my head. I turn and run.

CHAPTER NINETEEN
Chewing

DINNER IS THE opposite of what Amber expects. It's rowdy and loud, except for the silent retreat group, who sit at a separate table thoughtfully chewing their food. Still, they join in the dining hall hijinks with their eyes, winking across the table or nudging their neighbour when someone makes a joke or shows off some silly party trick.

Amber is stuck between a thin person with brittle brown hair and a woman wearing a bright pink hijab. Across from her is a senior who will not shut up for the love of God. They introduced themselves when Amber joined their table, but she doesn't care enough to remember their names.

The thin one stifles a laugh and the woman in the hijab nods before going off on a tirade about her preferred lyrical poets. The group is clearly comfortable with each other, and occasionally try to include Amber.

"How d'you like the food, Deb?" the senior asks as the woman in the hijab finishes a literary joke Amber does not understand.

"It's good," she says into her plate. Deb spears her fork into a pepper and scoops it into her mouth, taking her time chewing. Meanwhile, Amber formulates a plan to get away from this collection of crazies and into Room 22. She gives the hall a once over—none of the twenty or so people at dinner match the description Marius gave her. Very short black hair, heavyset, blue eyes, young lips…*What if she changed herself, bought a disguise?* she asked Marius before leaving, but he shook his head. Reena, whoever she is, wouldn't change a thing.

"The food here is amazing," the senior states. "Remember two days ago, what was that dish Reena made for us?"

"The roasted tofu and rice balls," the thin one sighs.

"Yes, with tomato sauce—"

"Reena?" Amber interrupts, a little too quickly. "Who's that?"

"The new cook—at least, I heard she was new," the woman in the hijab smiles.

The thin person nods vigorously. "Just showed up last week. She used to live here when she was a teenager, Carey told me."

"Oh, maybe she's related to Lin?"

"I don't think I've met her," Amber jumps into the conversation, hoping someone will help her out with a description.

The thin one is just about to take the bait when Carey glides over to them.

"Hey," Carey gives Amber-Deb a welcoming smile. "I'm going to need some help cleaning up after supper. Would any of you happen to be free?"

"I can help!" Amber shouts and then blushes. "I mean, I'd like to help. It's, it'd be n-nice to have something to do."

"Are you sure? It's your first night."

Deb nods and stares at her plate.

"Alright, then. Come to the kitchen when you're done out here. No rush, okay?"

Amber watches as Carey pushes open one of the double doors leading to the kitchen and lets it swing back behind them.

Pretty much done with her plate, Amber downs the rest of her iced tea, waiting another minute or two so as not to seem too eager.

When she pushes back her chair, the thin person asks, "Not staying for dessert?"

Deb makes some kind of excuse, which Amber is sure is polite and appropriately nervous, but her mind is on other things. Like what to say to Reena, or if she should talk to her at all. Befriending her could make getting into Room 22 easier. Maybe asking to borrow an extra towel, or wanting to talk about her recent trouble with her "partner." But Reena might be on her guard against strangers. She must know something's off if she's hiding out in the middle of nowhere.

"Is it okay if I...?" Deb says through the slight opening between the two doors leading into the kitchen.

"Come on in, Deb." Carey sets a dishwashing tray on the countertop.

Amber-Deb pushes the door inwards and slips inside before it swings back on her. The kitchen is unsurprising. A centre island inlaid with a stainless steel industrial sink. Granite countertops and wooden cupboards lining the walls. On one side of the room is a double oven and stove top piled with used saucepans, a silver sanitising unit loaded with dishwashing trays on the other. The fridge and deep freeze hum behind her. Before she got the job at *High Five*, she worked in the catering department at a sports club. Probably why this kitchen seems so familiar.

"Where's the cook?" Amber-Deb asks, realising that she and Carey are the only people in the kitchen.

"Oh, you mean Reena? Once she makes sure the food is okay, she usually eats in her room."

"Kind of stuck up." Amber-Deb waits for Carey's reaction.

"She cooks, we clean. I think it's a fair way of doing it, don't you?"

Amber-Deb shrugs, not wanting to make a thing of it. *At least I know when not to break into her room.*

"Now," Carey says with a generous amount of enthusiasm, "Do you want to wash the pots or run the dishwasher? I have some scraping brushes here, rice is a bitch to get off."

After the first sanitising round of pots and dishes, Carey sends Amber out into the dining hall with a spray bottle and a rag. The tables have cleared out for the most part. Only the silent retreaters remain, sitting on yoga mats in the corner. They pass a book around their circle, taking turns to read aloud.

"So much for a vow of silence," Amber mutters. At the same time, she knows that the reading is part of their retreat. She hasn't been to any kind of church since her mother made her go as a child, but she recognises the ritual of it all.

Their measured voices echo as Amber sprays vinegar water over the tables and wipes them down. *Two others, criminals, were also led out with him...*

Forgive them, they don't know what they're doing...

...and the guards cast lots for his body parts.

One of the criminals hurled insults…but the other rebuked him.

We are punished justly…but this person has done nothing wrong.

Amber finds herself in the kitchen, the door swinging shut behind her. She shakes her head as if breaking a trance, and tries to ignore the knot in her stomach.

#

Her borrowed hands pruned and sore from scrubbing, Amber-Deb finally says goodnight to Carey and heads to her room. The clock in the now-empty dining hall reads 8:47 pm. It's strange to think that she's been here for less than a day, has only eaten one meal here. Being Deb has already turned into a long eternity, and she's anxious to be on her own, to close the door and relax.

The hallway leading to the east bank of rooms is relatively empty. Amber walks by a person carrying a notebook and a blanket, but thankfully, they're one of the silent ones. She shuffles across the short pile carpet and passes under a wooden archway marked "20s". Room 22 looms on her left, marked by an eerie moment of anticipation: the thought of making it through the door, smuggling the package into Reena's belongings, and getting clean away. The thought of getting caught. The thought of making it in, but then having to fend off an unanticipated attack. All possible scenarios exist in the moment she passes Room 22.

But those thoughts can wait. The heavy hand of sleep pushes down on her eyelids. Amber-Deb unlocks her own door, number 28, and goes inside.

CHAPTER TWENTY
Helping Hand

I'VE BEEN RUNNING since Second Hand, since I heard the pack in wool coats shout at me to "Stop right there!"

My legs are failing, my lungs throwing in the towel. The alley walls curve in towards me, footsteps catching up in a thundering approach, like thousands of hands clapping or beating the arms of chairs. I wonder if anyone's watching, any gods or skids who just happen to be at their window. I will stop running and die alone.

"This way." I feel more than hear the words. An arm reaches out of a doorway, supports my shoulders, presses me towards a short concrete staircase.

"No..." I'm about to resist, but the voice—

"Crouch behind this," Adam whispers, sliding a cardboard box over the thin snow in front of us.

The footsteps rumble by like a train in the night.

"Hurry." Adam leads me up a rusted ladder bolted to the wall. We're up top now, too visible. Adam runs ahead and opens a red metal door.

In here, Adam motions. He looks down at the street as I get inside.

Adam shuts us in. We sit on the top step, the rest of the concrete stairs descending from our feet into darkness. My heart batters the inside of my chest. Our mouths release steam, the cold condensing our breath into transient clouds.

"Once we catch our breath, we can make our way out of the neighbourhood."

"They'll find the ladder," I say, starting to stand again, but he shakes his head.

"Door's locked from this side. They can't get in."

"How do you know? Was it locked before?"

Adam smiles, and the sheen of his skin catches me off-guard. I find myself looking at my hands, one slightly more tan than the other.

"I know my way around," he says simply.

I can't stop the shivering: it's so sudden, wavering through my skin—it *happens* to me, I can't—

"Are you cold?" His eyes wait steadily for me to answer.

"Must be the adrenaline wearing off." Bile rises in my throat but I push it under. "I don't understand what's happening."

"We'll work on figuring that out once we get home."

"Back to Jessica's?" A bite of panic tears through my throat. "I can't, that's where they want me to go—Jessica knows that I'm—that I'm—"

The warm pressure of Adam's hand passes across my back, back and forth, a wave drawing upshore and flowing back out into the sea.

The shivering shakes out of me, and I draw a deep breath. The exhale rushes out, takes some of the edge with it.

Standing, Adam offers me a hand up. "We'll figure it out." He pushes open the red door and leads me across the roof, down another ladder, into the alleys.

#

Jessica nearly has a fit. "I told you to go!"

The three of us stand in the living room, rigid and uncertain.

When we entered the apartment, Jessica was staring out at the city through the fogged-up patio door glass, but her whole body metamorphosed into a bird of prey the second I came into view.

Adam intercedes. "There's something very wrong—"

"How much did Marius pay you to spy on us?"

"Mom."

Her eyebrows crush down, reducing her gaze to a narrowed strip of anger.

I don't know what to say. I sit in the chair with the missing slat. Its frown is familiar against my back. Thank Christ Reena isn't here.

Adam places one of his broad hands on my shoulder. "Are you sure?" he asks me.

"Yes." *Let go, let go, let go…*

Adam's fingertips rest gently on my forehead, giving me a moment. Then he peels it back. He removes the front of my skull.

I keep my eyes on Jessica. She hasn't moved, but her mouth is wedged shut and her sharp shoulders heave. Her eyes are wide now. I hope the anger in them isn't for me.

"Put it back," she says, her voice shaking.

Adam reattaches my skull. I feel it click into place and settle until I'm no longer aware of it. My forehead smooths into its familiar gap, closing everything back in, including the circuit board wedged into my frontal lobe.

"Fuck." Jessica says it once, passing a hand through her white hair.

I take a steadying breath. "I didn't know."

"Of course you didn't," she growls, coming towards me. Adam shifts, but doesn't say anything. Maybe the back of the chair will swallow me before Jessica can tear me to shreds. She lifts her hands and I shut my eyes—

Her arms close around me, but there's no pain. Only warmth, the smell of coffee, and pressure on my back, my chest, my cheek as Jessica Fit holds me.

"I think I'm helping people, but then someone who really needs help shows up and I chase them away." Jessica releases the hug. "I'm so sorry."

"Okay," I say, trying to stay aloof from it all. But the hug, the machine in my brain, all of it is too much.

"Mom," Adam says, "have you seen anything like this before?"

Jessica looks at the art wall as if trying to find the answer in one of the bizarre paintings. She sighs. "When Nan's hand tried to attack me, it reminded me of a teen who used to come to the drop-in centre. His leg would get all jittery. Sometimes it would flail to the side without warning. Some of the other kids wouldn't go near him. I thought they were afraid of getting hit, but it was more than that. He couldn't control the leg at all. Eventually, he stopped wearing it altogether."

"I traded it in." I hold up my new hand. "This new one seems fine. It's safe now, right?"

Jessica crosses her arms. "It's not just that."

"You're right, you're right." Christ. What else is my body capable of?

She glances at Adam, then turns back to me. "Go home."

"You can't do this!" The words brim over like scalding water that I have to throw away as soon as possible. "They did this to me, to get to you or Reena, I don't know! Please. Help me, you owe me—"

"We have to get that thing out of you," she interrupts, "but I need some time to work out how to accomplish that."

"They'll come after me again," my voice shrinks.

Adam shakes his head. "I'll walk you home tonight. If anybody tries to follow you, I can get you out."

Jessica adds a *hmm*, agreeing. "If you're where you're supposed to be, I don't think they'll bother you. Go home, and pretend everything is normal."

"Home..." The word is unfamiliar now, some vague building with a kitchen and a bed. Will my mom be there? Is she even my mom? I start to crumble under the weight of the circuit board behind my forehead. I could be anyone.

Adam passes a hand across my back, like before. Jessica and her apartment come back into focus.

"See you tomorrow," she says, her voice warm again. Her eyes gleam, already ripping through the problem, already giving me a shred of hope.

#

It isn't even midnight yet. I can't remember the last time I was home this early. Mom is at the kitchen island, drinking from a glass. Vodka, is my immediate guess, but then I remember she hasn't had a drink in almost two years. At least, I think I do.

"Oh, you're back," she says, both of her eyes turning towards me in unison. I'm still not used to it. I keep expecting one of them to roll slowly outwards, her tendency to multitask.

Sitting on the stool across from her, I rest my forearms on the pristine countertop. "How was your day?"

She pauses slightly as she reaches for her glass. "Fine. Busy, actually, but fine."

"Mom."

"Yes?"

"Who paid for your eye replacement?"

"What do you mean? I did, of course." She laughs in her throat, like I've made some kind of rude joke. "You see anybody else around here working for a living? Oh, I know you have that part-time job at the sunglasses stand, but that money's for your education."

"I thought you couldn't afford it before. That's why you never changed it."

"Oh, didn't I tell you? We broke a sales record last month, and each of us got a little bonus in our paycheck. When I say little, I mean considerable." She takes a moment to throat laugh again. "I got the bonus and I thought, it's my turn to have a little something, you know? We're good and taken care of, so why don't I get a little something out of it?" Her double-eyed gaze turns serious. "Tell me that, child of mine. You have put me through some serious shit, you know, and I thought, I deserve something nice out of this. And you know what? I don't care that you don't approve. I don't care that you are off all day doing shit all, and I don't care that having you here has completely taken over my life—"

Her mouth shuts up the rest. Both of her eyes roll off me and carry her over to the fridge. "You want anything?" she says, suddenly sweet. The blonde bun on the back of her head keeps track of me like another eye.

A heaviness settles into my stomach. I remember to breathe. "No. Thanks." The distance from the stool to the floor is uncrossable, until my bare feet curl against the cold linoleum. "Goodnight, Mom."

"'Night, sweetheart. Have a good sleep." She keeps her head in the fridge until I leave. I hear the insulated door seal shut as I climb the stairs to my room.

Is it my room? Standing in the centre, I take in every detail. A plaid shirt hangs from a checkmark-shaped hook screwed to the back of the door. A blue and grey checkered comforter covers the queen-sized bed which protrudes coffin-style from the middle of the far wall. A nightstand on one side, a varnished wooden dresser on the other. The walls are a navy blue, bare. No posters, no photos, no framed accomplishments. Nothing that lists my name or shows me what I look like. As if the room I can remember from my childhood up until about two years ago has been stripped of its personality, its history. Did I do that? Did my Mom? Did someone else?

I take the wallet from my jeans pocket. Inside is $50 in cash and two cards: a debit card featuring a raised string of silver numbers, an expiry date, and a scribbled, indecipherable signature on the back; and the ID I used to get into *Beauty Mark*.

Birth Name: Rowan Sylvia Arlo Hain

Birth Date: September 16, 12,002

The dotted lines where I can write in my chosen name and pronouns are blank.

I return the cards to my wallet.

There is a circuit board in my brain. There is a circuit board in my brain. There is a circuit board in my brain.

I could remove it. Stand in front of a mirror, peel off my own forehead, the skull plate, wrench the fucking thing out. But years of school and PSAs and common sense telling me that self-surgery is dangerous and should only be left to trained professionals gets in my way.

Instead, I tip the lamp back on its base. Slide the Polaroid free. Laying on the bed, I stare up at the laughing figure with blue hair, trying to remember.

CHAPTER TWENTY-ONE
Cybernetics

WHEN I ARRIVE at the apartment, the door is unlocked. Inside, music plays, some kind of jazz. Two familiar voices waft around the corner. I breathe deep into my chest, let it rise and fall, check in that I'm still here, still me. I reach through the tips of my fingers, the ends of my toes. My stomach clenches beneath the loose front of the camo jacket.

One voice says something, the other laughs. I pass through the entryway, nervous. What if Jessica changed her mind and kicks me out for good? I wouldn't blame her. Who knows what else my body has been programmed to do.

"How lovely to see you again!" Mr. Snaff booms from the chair with the missing slat. He smiles diagonally, looking down over his chin. He's wearing scuffed brown loafers, tweed pants, and a lime green turtleneck.

A portable record player sits on the fold-out table next to him, a vinyl spinning inside the stylized suitcase. He sets down an album sleeve and waves me over to the table. "It's been a few days, hasn't it! I hear you've had some trouble since we last met."

I take the end seat, let my head respond.

"Well, I've got just the thing!" Mr. Snaff winks and lifts the needle from the spinning record. He lowers his torso slightly to allow him a better view of the grooves. After a moment, he gingerly sets the needle down and a new song begins. "Beautiful, this one," he says, leaning back in his chair.

Jessica appears from the back hallway with a duffel bag, her feet falling in time with the bassline. "As you can see, I've asked Mr. Snaff to help with your predicament."

"I don't know how jazz music is going to help," I reply.

"Oh, I only brought these for us to enjoy!" Mr. Snaff exclaims. "But if it's time to work, let's get to it!" He stands and stretches his thick cylindrical arms over his head, bouncing slightly on his toes until his back cracks. "Ah, much better!"

"What should I...?"

"You can stay right where you are and relax." Jessica sets an empty bowl on the table before handing Mr. Snaff the duffel bag. "Mr. Snaff is very skilled with this kind of thing."

"What, brain implants?"

"Biology and electronics!" he exclaims. "I oversee the robotics club, you know, such a fascinating area of study!" He plucks a very small set of pliers out of the bag. "Now. Our first step is to gather data. Jess told me all about what happened, but I'm going to take a look and see what kind of tech we're dealing with. If you could just turn your chair to face the wall... excellent! Ready?"

I readjust my back against the chair and tuck my hair behind my ears. "Yeah sure," I say, almost accustomed to people removing my forehead.

"Here we go!" Mr. Snaff stands on my right side, listing sideways to get a clear view of my forehead. He smells like shoe polish and old books, unthreatening.

I let him take away my forehead, the front of my skull. He exclaims, like everyone else before, that there's something in there that shouldn't be. A machine of some kind, though he calls it something else.

"Cybernetics," I can hear his voice, but my eyes only see as far as his turtleneck. "A site for a program to communicate with the brain. I've never seen one this advanced!"

"What kind of program, Mr. Snaff?" Jessica asks from beyond the wall of lime green.

"Could be that there are certain stimuli or information that this system is feeding into the brain. And if I can just—" The small pliers squeak as he works them around something. "Ah! There you are!" A metallic ring as Mr. Snaff drops it into the bowl. "A tracker!"

"That's how they knew you were at the secondhand store," Jessica's voice reaches me.

Mr. Snaff moves to the table, freeing my view. The art wall comes into focus, paintings of figures with melting eyes or confused limbs. I feel sorry for them, because I am one of them now. I know what it's like to have a body I have no control over.

"This machine could also be repressing information," Mr. Snaff muses as he sifts through the duffel bag. Metal clinks against metal. Could be anything in there. Saws, welding torches, scalpels, needles. A lump rises in my throat, but I clear it before it cuts me off.

"I'm going to try manipulating the circuitry," he says a little bit louder, to let me know he's talking to me now, not just himself. Wanting some kind of permission.

I clear my throat again. "Okay."

"You're being very brave!" he praises me, and I smile just a little. Mr. Snaff is possibly the most ridiculous human I have ever met. And Christ, I like him.

Mr. Snaff reaches over with both hands, holding small pliers and another tool that rushes past my face too fast to really register.

I hold my eyes on the art wall, finding a picture of a genderfluid god, surrounded in a halo of ripped up book pages. Pastel waves radiate around the face, a mosaic of glossy photo shards, two kaleidoscopic eyes, lips half pink and half black, lined cheeks, wearing a freckled nose and deep purple forehead. I almost relax.

Nausea hits. Sweat beads on my upper lip, my chest heaves, and all the lights go out as the memory surfaces and swallows me whole.

CHAPTER TWENTY-TWO
Spare Parts

THEY GOT ME at the transit terminal; hands clamping my arms, the smell of sweat and boutique cologne emanating from their wool coats. I'd heard rumours about these people. They took what they could from some, straight-up killed others. Once you reached 18, you were fair game for those parts vultures.

I wake up in a room I don't recognize. Nothing notable about it; no windows, no pictures—just white walls, and a faint hum from somewhere behind me. I try to move, but I'm strapped to a chair. No way out.

Someone watching, standing close by. A suit, gelled-back hair, sunglasses. His teeth gleam like a dozen animal eyes.

"You're no good to us this way." Marius glides up to me. "We're going to make a couple of changes. What do you think? New chin? Younger, of course. We'll keep you a blonde, if you prefer."

"Don't get me wrong," I say, pushing down the screaming fear. "I appreciate the offer. Really. But you see, I'm kinda attached to my current model."

"Funny," he deadpans. "This won't take long."

"Going to use me for parts?" I let the burning in my throat spit fire into my words.

His mouth widens into a grotesque grin, the bridge of his upturned nose buckling. "I want you to watch this film and try to relax."

The straps across my chest make it hard to breathe. He's trying to get me to the point of passing out, not quite. Just enough to make me loose.

Marius grips my chin and shoves a tablet into my mouth. It fizzes on my tongue, dissolves away.

The lights dim. A door closes and bolts shut. I send awareness down to my fingers, to each toe. My throat tightens; my intestines stiffen. Somewhere in my skull, that's me, looking out.

An empty screen projects onto the bare wall. The film starts, a sequence of landscapes, colourful fields, nothing to distract, nothing to draw me out too much.

"The Rockies…Angel Falls…you can see the Grand Canyon from space…" I narrate each scene aloud, to keep a hold on something, anything to keep me from going under.

But I lose my grip. Darkness flickers, heavy eyelids closing out the images. Edges of me dissolving. He'll take anything he wants.

"Christ," I say, one last time.

CHAPTER TWENTY-THREE
Heartbeat

"HOW ARE YOU feeling?"

The memory clears like fog, leaving a cold chill on my skin. "Is it gone?"

Mr. Snaff looks down his nose, compassionately. "Do you want to see it?"

I shake my head once and stop, nausea threatening the back of my throat.

"I checked for your ID chip while I was in there," Mr. Snaff continues in an uncharacteristically subdued voice. "Looks like they left that alone, thank heavens."

The phantom weight of the mechanism pulls my forehead forward. I stare at the hardwood floor, each breath echoing in my ears. "I think I should lie—"

When I open my eyes, the ceiling is half-shadowed, lamplight illuminating the corner of the room. I can make out each of the corners where the walls and ceiling meet. A smaller room than I was in before, one where I am on a bed and my whole body is warm.

Sitting up, the first thing I notice is the blanket over my legs. I pass my hand over it. The fabric is as soft as cat fur.

My neck prickles, but when I turn to the figure in the corner, it's no one at all. Just a dress on a grey woollen torso next to the sewing machine. This must be Reena's bedroom. I spend five minutes staring at the wall-mounted shelf above me, the bottom of it unfinished wood.

The sensation slowly builds, a deep sour pressure in my abdomen. I have to piss. I flip the blanket from my legs and place my feet on the floor. I'm still in the same clothes I passed out in: thick winter socks, a pair of sweatpants, and a worn t-shirt.

Something's different. I can sense it in the air—a quiet intimacy. Like I'm the only one in the world awake. One hundred percent present. Yesterday and the day ahead exist as if in a dream.

I feel like I've been dreaming. Of course I was. No evil contraption in my head, no child's disembodied fingers. Impossible things. I must've stayed the night after returning Jessica's mouth.

I open the door into the hall. The lights are off in the rest of the apartment; almost all of the other doors are closed. I head for the bathroom.

Once inside, I flip on the lightswitch, lock the door. Pretty cosy in here, I think, undoing my pants and doing my business. I have a moment of indecision, staring at the yellow bowl. If I flush, will it wake everyone up? But I'm a guest, I remember. Better to erase that I was here at all.

The toilet flushed and my hands washed, I venture back into the shadowy hallway. My mouth is extremely dry, like, parched levels. I continue down the hall, into the main area of the apartment.

Streetlight bleeds in through the patio door and the window over the kitchen sink. I guess it's around four in the morning and am rewarded by 4:22 on the glowing stove clock. Using the time's dim green light, I take a glass down from the cupboard and open the tap, overfilling the glass before I remember to turn off the water. I chug half the glass, breaking to breathe.

That's when I see it. The shoebox on the counter.

I set the glass down. Wipe the moisture from my lips with the back of my hand. I know what's inside the shoebox. But if I'm right, it means that all of it happened. That impossible things have happened to me.

Everything freezes. Only my eyes feel alive, flicking to the shoebox and then away, panic curling in my stomach.

My feet carry me to the counter. My hands, one slightly more tan than the other, reach for the shoebox. The cardboard is rough on my fingertips.

I can go back to bed, I tell my hands. This can all still be a dream.

But my hands do not want dreams. They lift the lid free.

Inside is a glossy panel the size of a stick of gum, wires bristling into silver discs and gold-pricked chips that bloom out from it like robot flowers.

It's the circuit board from inside my head.

My hands replace the lid and then hold each other as if for comfort. My feet take me blessedly away, through the hall and back into Reena's room, with the warm lamp on the desk, the finished wedding dress, the safe bed.

I pull the soft blanket up all the way over me. Without a protective case for my eyes, this is the next best thing.

My heartbeat drums through the dark. I listen as it slows, until I am sure that I will fall asleep.

#

"How are you feeling? Mr. Snaff assured me that all you needed was a good night's sleep."

"Bit of a headache."

"Coffee?" Jessica's wearing green slacks and a black sweater along with a stained-glass scarf, her short, white hair brushed back from her face. Her dark eyes have tired rings under them, and her cheeks sag.

"Looks like you didn't sleep much." I accept the full mug she hands me, and scan the countertop. The shoebox is nowhere to be seen.

She *hmms* in reply, and pours some coffee for herself.

"It all happened, right?" I ask. "The thing in my brain?"

Her eyes tighten, and she nods, replacing the coffee pot on the warming element.

"Shit."

Drawing a cutting board from a cupboard, Jessica sets it on the empty counter and turns away to open the fridge.

The city fills the frost-edged window over the sink. Cars and buses crawl along the road. Pedestrians follow the sidewalk, their faces obscured by scarves and winter hoods. I wonder what they're thinking as they go wherever they're going.

The hum of the fridge closing draws me back. Jessica arranges a bunch of carrots and a netted bag of celery next to the cutting board. "Do you know who did it?"

"I had a dream the other night...I think it was Marius."

Jessica frowns and begins to cut up the vegetables. "Remember that teenager I told you about, with the leg that was out of control? I didn't tell you everything. I suspected that there was more to the leg's behaviour than just a bad connection. I got the kid to admit that Marius was paying him to use the leg. Some kind of experimental part. Grossly unethical. I reported it to the police, but there wasn't enough evidence. The kid wouldn't testify. It was a real mess. That was about five years ago." Her jaw tenses. She brushes the bad ends off of the cutting board. "You can go to the police. I'll back you up for what it's worth."

I take a carrot stick from the pile on the cutting board and take a bite.

Jessica sweeps the bad ends into a compost bin that she replaces under the sink. "Marius thinks he's untouchable. A god who can reorganise the world, take parts from the vulnerable and sell them to people who already have wealth and status and food in abundance. It's f—" She looks over at me, hand poised to strip the word right off, and reconsiders. "It's fucked up."

"Proud of you," I tease.

"Yeah, well." She smiles, fiercely. "It was deserved." She pauses for a moment, then pulls a couple cans of tuna and a bowl down from a cupboard. She fishes a can opener out of the pitcher of cooking utensils. "Would you mind getting the bread?"

I tuck the end of the carrot stick in my mouth like a cigarette, and follow her pointing to the slim pantry closet. Finding the breadbox, I pull a loaf free and place it next to the cutting board. "Was I.. .programmed? To follow you, I mean."

"I think so." She fits the can opener over the tuna and cranks it open. "To keep track of Reena probably. Something to do with the fingers. Or maybe Marius had something else planned that went awry when you traded your hand away."

My new right hand stays relaxed on my knee. "What if there are…other parts of me that he changed?"

"The hospital could be a good place to start," Jessica says as she places the serrated can lid into the sink. "Do you remember the last time you had a check-in?"

I shake my head.

"We can go after lunch." She washes her hands and unplugs her cell phone from the outlet by the coffeemaker. "I'll ask my friend if we can borrow her car."

#

Full up with tuna sandwiches and carrot sticks, I sit in the corner while Jessica wipes down the counters. I pivot my head from side to side, feel my hair settle against my cheek. I notice how the air I inhale presses outward against the walls of my lungs, how my ribs lift to make room.

I squint at the patio doors framing the midday city as my mind combs through a dozen garbled memories:

"Nan," my mom calls down from a window.

"Nan!" a panicked voice echoes up an alley.

"Nan…" an alto voice in the dark, low with longing.

Their names, on the tip of my tongue, the cutting edge of consciousness.

On some level, it doesn't really matter that I can't remember them. People change their names all the time, almost as often as body parts. Some names are given, some names chosen. ID chips are for medical and legal matters, while ID cards exist to tell the world your names. But my ID card is blank where my chosen name should be. Not even that's significant, given what I know now. Marius must've told the bullet-eyed bouncer to let me into the *Beauty Mark* regardless.

Even though I know it's gone, I can still feel the circuit board hooked up to my frontal lobe. But brains don't feel. The hub for all the senses, the brain is unaware of heat, light, pain. All the same, the fear of it digs deeper into me, somewhere in my head, my "I". I'm ringed in, trying to push through, kept from fully knowing myself.

Adam settles on the hardwood across from me. "You're in Reena's spot," he notes.

I turn in my seat, study the place where the walls and ceiling join. "Feels safe here."

He folds in his tall person legs, placing his palms over the thin knees of his cargo pants. "I heard you had quite the day."

I incline my chin, feeling the weight of my forehead as I nod.

"How are you doing?"

I really like Adam's face. I mean, once you get over the nameless plane of his skin, the colourless irises, the translucent lips, it's pleasant to look at. One of his eyelids droops slightly, a comfortable glance. Smile lines are starting to carve their way into his narrow cheeks. His forehead is short and furrowed, like it used to be bigger but got stuck that way from constant thoughtfulness. Maybe he reminds me of someone I can't remember. The overwhelming feeling Adam's face brings is nostalgia. A sense of something I've lost, but not entirely let go of.

"I'm okay," I finally reply, trying to mimic his quiet smile. "At least I know."

"Know what happened?"

"Yeah."

"Do you think it will change anything?"

"What do you mean?"

Adam shifts his crossed legs, straightening his back. "How you think about yourself. What you're going to do next."

"What I'm going to do next...?"

"Yeah."

I don't know any more than I did before, not really. My memory bank of the past two years seems to be in the red. And before that? I don't know which memories are mine, if any. Maybe they're all implants. I don't know the whys behind it. Why me? What for? I only have my second-hand hand. The only part I can be sure is mine. Something I chose. "I'll just...try to remember what I can."

Her toque already on, Jessica comes out of the kitchen, one hand grabbing her trench coat from the back of a chair, the other picking something out of the metal bowl on the counter.

"Here," she drops the small round tracker in my hand. "Might want to keep that on you."

"Do you think they know?"

"All we can do is hope that they don't. Keep acting as normal as possible."

"Right," I stand up, slipping the tracker into my coat pocket. "Normal. Whatever that is."

Adam's face brightens in agreement.

CHAPTER TWENTY-FOUR
A Clear Blue Eye

AMBER RECLINES IN the room's cushioned chair, her feet up on the windowsill. Working her fingers through the holes of the crocheted throw, she feels where the wool has gone soft from multiple washes and years of use. Pulling it tighter around her shoulders, she stares out over the smooth acre of snow behind the retreat centre leading to a barren lake, iced-over and rippled from the wind. Past that is the stark treeline, pines all jagged, stabbing upwards like a row of open switchblades.

The sudden glow from her phone draws her attention. Reception here hovers around one bar, and sometimes kicks over to roaming, which doesn't matter so long as Marius reimburses her when she gets back.

One more day

The time stamp reads 9:01 am, at least where she is. 11:01 from Cam's perspective. Amber wonders if he's anxious for her to be home, or if Marius told him to send the message as a reminder—or as a warning.

Whatever, she says to herself, *I have a handle on the situation.*

The plan is simple. She'll wait until about an hour before mealtime, when Reena usually leaves her room to prepare dinner. Then, once the hallway is clear, she'll slip into Room 22 and secrete the package somewhere in Reena's belongings. That way, it won't be found right away, maybe not even until after Deb disappears, whisked away in a white van, never to be seen again.

A wave of uneasy excitement hits Amber in the gut. Finally, she's doing more than preparing the store deposit or printing out inventory lists. This is the real work. She's getting a taste of what really goes on, just like Marius promised.

#

There's a knock on the door. Amber-Deb sits up, one hand reaching for her phone. 3:38 pm. Just under half an hour until Reena leaves her room. Another knock pulls her from where she's been laying over the covers, hovering between sleep and visualising the various outcomes of her mission.

"Just a sec!" she says to whoever is on the other side of the door. Her hands automatically readjust a bobby pin to secure a loose strand of hair out of her face. She runs a quick check: clothes, face, body parts all in order. She opens the door.

It's the woman in the pink hijab, only today her face is framed by turquoise, the overlap of fabric secured with a silver brooch in the shape of a feather. "Hello," she smiles.

"Hey," Amber-Deb replies, more like a question than a greeting.

"I'm on my way to the yoga session, do you want to come?"

"Well, I don't, I don't know," Amber says, remembering to make Deb sound as pathetic as possible. "I've never done yoga before, I don't think I should—"

"It's very chill," she continues cheerfully, "Lin instructs, xe's really good. And it might help, you know? Just something to pass the time."

While the woman waits for Deb's reply, Amber is struck by how convenient this could turn out to be. Yoga could be an alibi. She could sneak out mid-session, drop the package in Reena's room, and be back in downward dog before anyone notices that she even left.

"That, that would be good," Amber-Deb replies. She makes a show of looking down at her clothes. "Are these, is what I'm wearing okay?"

She nods encouragingly. "Yes, as long as you're comfortable. Oh, and I know we met at dinner yesterday, but in case you need a refresher, I'm Karima."

"Deb." Amber-Deb joins Karima in the hallway, closing the door behind her. "How did you know where to find me?"

"I told Carey I wanted to invite you, and they gave me your room number. I don't mean to intrude."

"It's okay," Deb says. Amber internally screams—all that sneaking around trying to find out Reena's room number and she could've just *asked*?

Whatever, she tells herself as she falls in step with Karima. *You did what you had to.*

"So, what brings you to the middle of nowhere?" Amber-Deb makes the joking tone flop on purpose.

Still, Karima smiles. "Isn't it like being on a different planet? I've been here almost two weeks and I don't miss the internet at all! Maybe a little. But it's been really good for my book."

"You're on a writing retreat?"

"It's an I-needed-some-time-on-my-own-to-finish-my-book-without-distractions kind of trip, so basically, yes. What about you?"

Amber stops walking and makes Deb's hands crimp the hem of her sweater. "I, I left my partner, and needed somewhere…somewhere safe."

"That's really brave of you," Karima says, offering her hand if Deb needs it.

Amber-Deb stares at the light grey carpet. A feeling of nausea floods over from Deb into Amber, but it means something completely different. While Deb is feeling anxious and afraid, Amber is feeling guilt.

Shut up, she berates herself, *you're not doing anything wrong.*

Karima lowers her hand. They continue into the dining area. The tables have been moved to one side to make room for around twenty yoga mats. A couple of the silent retreaters sit cross-legged, their hands resting on their knees or stretching overhead. Amber-Deb and Karima choose two mats at the back of the yoga space and wait for Lin to arrive.

Amber nods to herself. She has a clear view of the double doors leading into the kitchen. The round windows are still dark. Reena won't be able to get in without her noticing.

"What's your book about?" Amber-Deb asks Karima, hoping to avoid any more references to her 'domestic troubles.'

"Are you asking to be polite, or do you want the involved play-by-play I only save for the truly interested?"

A laugh escapes from Amber. "If I said I was truly interested, would you believe me?"

Karima shrugs and pretends to consider Deb's sincerity. "Sure. I'd give you a chance."

"Try me," Amber says, before sinking back into Deb. God, it felt good to talk to someone, as herself. Only a day and a half since her arrival, but she misses her own hands. Funny, since she's saving up for that floor model back at *High Five*. And her third eye, she's missed depending on it for another way of seeing things. How things often aren't one thing or the other, but somewhere in-between.

"...she's this extremely introverted character, but I need her to do something out of the ordinary." Karima stops mid-synopsis, turning to Amber-Deb. "What do you think?"

Amber-Deb continues her train of thought. "People aren't one thing or the other, right? Maybe she can be somewhere in the middle. Willing to take a risk, for the right reason."

"That could work... I mean, it *is* right before they find out who the murderer is, she'd still be motivated to find out what happened." Karima takes her phone from the pocket of her hoodie. "I'm going to write that down before I forget..."

As Karima types, Reena enters the dining room. Short black hair, imposing bulk, ice-blue eyes set straight ahead. Her bottom lip protrudes slightly in a juvenile pout. Just as Marius described her.

Not sparing a glance for the yoga set-up, Reena disappears into the kitchen.

"Shit!" Amber-Deb exclaims, making a show out of patting down her pockets. "Where's my phone?"

Karima looks up from her notes. "Do you want help looking for it?"

"I probably just left it in my room. I forgot...my lawyer, they're supposed to call...I'll be right back."

"I'll save your mat for you."

"Thanks."

Karima smiles and turns back to her phone.

#

Room 22.

The lock is like hers, a simple in-handle slot. Amber quickly loosens the bobby pin from her hair, her other hand gripping the paper bag rolled up in her sweater pocket. It takes a long 30 seconds for her to spring the lock. Her hand shakes as she replaces the pin and enters the room.

Stop it, she tells her borrowed hand, but the tremor continues until the door secures behind her.

Amber quickly searches the room. The bed is made, blue curtains secured with ties on either side of the window. A yellow, hardcover book sits on the nightstand. Reena's clothes are folded into one bureau drawer. A suitcase sits neatly behind the door.

Deciding on the drawer, Amber's fingers flip through the folded shirts like stacked records. Pulling the top of a red hoodie free, she stuffs the paper bag down its throat.

As she closes the drawer, everything comes to a grinding halt. Someone is turning the door handle. Someone is going to come in. Someone is going to find her in a room that isn't hers.

Come on, Deb, what are you doing? What do you want? They're going to ask you, what the hell are you doing in here?

Amber's alter-ego huddles in the corner of her consciousness. Her body mirrors Deb, sinking down against the wall behind the bed, crushing her shoulder up against the wooden nightstand.

The latch clicks. The door swings open.

Amber holds her breath.

Reena comes into the room with glazed eyes that do not see presences, not absences, not the in-between of Amber-Deb huddling in the corner. She turns and presses the door closed with both hands.

Amber sneaks a small breath as Reena's back approaches her and topples onto the bed. The edge of the mattress lifts from the added weight and rests under Amber's nose. The smell of powdered detergent and the polyester duvet fills her nostrils, threatening to stifle her. She doesn't move. She waits, as she always does, for an opportunity to present itself.

If Reena returned for a nap, Amber can crawl around the bed as soon as her breathing settles into a slow, even rhythm. Or, is this simply a short break? After all, Reena can't have made food for over twenty people in under ten minutes, right? Either way, Reena has no reason to turn around; she only has to get up and proceed out of the room the way she came in. A few minutes later, Amber will be clear to escape.

The mattress springs creak as Reena sits up, straight-backed and alert. Amber holds back a groan as the head of short black hair pivots to reveal an ear. Half a cheek. A clear blue eye.

Frozen, Amber shivers as its gaze washes over her.

"You're not who I expected," Reena says.

Amber decides that now would be a good time to leave. She stands as well as she can in the small space, banging her shoulder against the nightstand. Before Amber can move past the end of the bed, Reena gets to her feet and plants herself in front of the door, her arms crossed.

"I'd like to talk to you before you go." Reena's voice is even, unsurprised.

Deb holds stock still as Amber considers the situation. Reena takes up too much space to get by easily. Her legs are tree trunks: impossible to push past. The window overlooking the frozen lake isn't a useful option either. A double pane of glass and a metal screen bars her from the expansive snowscape beyond.

"You're working for Marius. Probably going to find another child's finger in this room somewhere, am I right? Do you even know what you're doing?"

"Another finger?" Amber swallows. She pictures the finger with the sparkly purple nail floating in the jar.

"Don't you wonder why Marius didn't just come himself? Easy enough for him to change." Reena's eyes narrow. "Anything feminine offends him, you know. He never found the balance in himself." Reena takes a deep breath and relaxes her arms. "Life is the balance, the co-existence, the variety of in-betweens. Men like him only use the feminine as a tool, when it suits them. Do you understand what I'm telling you?"

Amber's head spins, her strange hands clenching the hem of her borrowed sweater, her borrowed life.

Reena's face falls, fatigue gathering around her eyes. "That's all." Moving away from the door, she settles on the edge of the mattress, her shoulders bowed.

Deb's body carries Amber out into the hallway. Her shoulder aches all the way to her room.

Amber sends a text to Cam, then lays on top of the duvet, her heart pounding from her run-in with Reena. What did she mean, all that balance nonsense? That's what places like this did to you, made you say things that didn't make sense.

Amber picks at her fingernail. Marius, using her? She's just doing her job. She went in, delivered the package, got it done. What's wrong with that?

Within the hour, Amber climbs into the backseat of a white van and slides the heavy metal door shut, leaving Deb and her questions behind.

CHAPTER TWENTY-FIVE
Check-In

ONCE WE REACH the hospital, Jessica and I are directed to the non-emergency waiting room, where we sit in uncomfortable red bucket seats bolted to the floor. A wall-mounted screen plays benign reviews of small-town gardens intercut with facts about chia seed and how best to take care of body parts in storage.

Keep detached parts in sealed cases to prevent infections and mould … … … After attaching a part, give your body a few hours to adjust before doing any major activity such as driving or playing a sport … … … If you break a bone, see a doctor first …

Flashes of the last time I was at the hospital fit together into a jagged memory. Two years ago, I think, right after Mom's rehab. My annual check-in. Mom was high on life, flirting with the jaundiced person across the waiting room. In the examination office, her honeyed attitude turned sour as she complained to the doctor how lazy I was, how I didn't appreciate her or give her any financial help. The doctor humoured her as he studied me. Like I was a taxidermied animal on display.

The TV shows another tranquil garden.

If you lose a part, or suspect one has been removed without your consent, report to your local hospital or police station as soon as possible ...

The ticker leaves a trail of burning ellipses behind. Bile pushes up my throat. I try to focus on the things around me, root myself into the present: Jessica's doing a crossword and we're the only ones in the waiting area and there was an implant in my brain but it's gone now.

The bile settles into a more manageable stomach knot. I clench my mismatched hands. There's nothing to be afraid of. I'll ask the doctor how my new parts are doing, they'll check everything. I'm going to be okay.

"Hain?" A voice announces, and I look up from my hands. Hain's the last name on my ID card.

"Here!" I propel myself out of the chair.

Jessica gives me an encouraging wave and returns to her crossword. Even if I wanted her to come with, only family members are allowed.

A nurse wearing teal scrubs patterned over in shells and starfish leads me through the examination hallway. "In this one, please," the nurse says, writing something on a clipboard and leaving it in a clear plastic holder on the door.

I go into the room and hop up on the padded bench. The long white sheet of paper protecting it crinkles under my butt.

The doctor comes in right away, holding the clipboard. "You dropped by at a good time," e says, "usually you'd be in here for half an hour before I could see you."

"Lucky, I guess."

The doctor's wiry, bronze eyebrows stick up past eir matching hairline. E scans the clipboard chart with a pert *hrmm*.

"You missed your last check-in, it looks like. I'm afraid if it happens again, we'll have to issue a fine and a mandatory follow-up."

"Okay."

"Is there anything bothering you, anything you'd like me to look at while you're here?" Eir golden eyes exude bedside manner.

"Just, I have some new parts, want to make sure they're all up to standard."

"We can do a scan if that'll make you feel more comfortable. No vertigo, dissociation, panic attacks?"

"No," I lie.

"Stand against this wall, please. Try to stay still."

I hold my breath as the medical-grade bioscanner buzzes behind my head, moving down my back all the way to my heels.

The doctor stands at a little fold-out desk. E pulls a monitor out from the wall. "It looks like you've made a lot of changes to your face, a new hand…am I missing anything?"

"What about my forehead?" Maybe they'll see something from the implant—

"Everything looks good and healthy. No bad connections, no neural deterioration. I think we can consider this check-in a success."

The knot in my stomach relaxes. I take a deep breath.

"While you're here, should I verify your ID chip? Do I need to update your name or pronouns?"

"What's on there right now?" Not a strange question. After all, a lot can change in two years.

"Looks like...Oh, that's odd. I can only see your birth name and date of birth." E types, taps the screen. "Very odd indeed. Well, I'll make a note on your file, see if this happens the next time you come in. Probably a simple glitch, nothing to worry about. What should I put in for your chosen name and pronouns?"

"I think I'll just leave it the way it is for now."

The doctor's eyebrows buck up like frizzy horses but are quickly reined in. "Legally, I have to accept your decision," e says with something like a sigh. "But please remember that if you want to add a name and pronoun between now and your next check-in, it'll cost you an administrative fee at City Hall."

"I understand."

"Alright then." The doctor swipes a finger across the screen and folds it back into the wall. "Everything's in good shape. We'll see you in a year."

Jessica looks up from her crossword as I re-enter the waiting room. She raises an eyebrow. "And?"

"I'm good. No more surprise parts."

We make our way to the exit and pause momentarily as the automatic door to the street slides open.

"Do you feel any different?" Jessica asks.

"I like knowing. The doctor didn't notice anything strange about my brain, except..."

"What?"

"My chosen name and pronouns aren't listed on my chip."

We reach the parking lot. The borrowed Jeep is a couple of stalls in. I peel around the back to the passenger side. It's an old vehicle, but the black paint has a healthy sheen to it.

We drive without speaking for a while, Jessica humming small notes along with the radio. "No Name," she says suddenly.

"Like the cat?"

"Yeah. I haven't seen him in a couple of days."

I know what she's asking. "I told the doctor not to add anything."

"I didn't want to pry."

"I don't know who I am anymore," I say, keeping my voice in check. "I want to try and find out."

She nods and weaves the Jeep through a gang of long hauler trucks.

I take out the card with my birth name and birthdate. "'Rowan Sylvia Arlo Hain.' This has to be my real ID. They called me Hain at the doctor's office, it lined up with the birth name on my chip. And I remember my Mom's birth name being Sylvia, I'm pretty sure."

"What about your other parent?"

"Arlo? I don't them remember so well." My brain seems to have peeled that memory completely away.

Jessica glances over. "We can call you No Name, if you like."

"Like the cat?"

We both laugh as Jessica noses the Jeep through traffic.

When we get back to the apartment, Adam is sitting on the counter with his legs hanging down. He's eating a piece of toast, studying the screen of a battered flip phone that looks about a thousand years old.

"Just heard from Reena." He brushes some crumbs from his sweater.

"Is she okay?" Jessica asks.

"Doesn't say. Just wants us to know she's taking the next train and will be back in a couple of days."

"She wasn't there very long."

"Someone found her at the retreat centre." Adam closes the phone and tucks it into the bulky pocket of his cargo pants. "She won't tell me anything else."

"I'm calling her." Jessica takes her own cell phone from her pocket and disappears into the back hall.

"So," Adam's worried expression relaxes as he turns his attention to me. "How was the doctor?"

"Everything looks good."

"That's good." He takes a couple more bites of toast.

"Yeah, but weird thing is, my ID chip didn't have a record of my chosen name or pronouns."

"That is weird," he says, voice muffled by crumbs.

"I don't mind, to be honest. I wouldn't want a doctor to give me my identity anyway."

Adam nods. "You can decide for yourself." He finishes the toast, brushes off the rest of the sweater crumbs. He doesn't have to jump down from the counter, more like he just stands, lowering his feet a couple of inches and pushing himself off the counter. He's tall and thin, and although his oversized hoodie hides most of his angles, his sharp shoulders could give Jessica's a run for their money.

"Did you ever," I say, feeling bold, "change your name? I mean, you seem like you've always been Adam, if you know what I mean."

"I've changed it a couple times," he says thoughtfully. "When I was a kid I thought Maximillian was the coolest name ever, so that's what I went by.

And when I moved in here, I decided I needed something new, 'cause life was different, you know? So when Jessica took me for my first check-in probably since birth, I told them to change my chosen name to Jeremy. But once I settled in here, and felt comfortable, I decided on Adam. It feels *right* to hear people call me Adam, if that makes sense."

I nod, wondering how to find that sense of rightness in myself.

"I've always gone by he/him, though. In high school, lots of my classmates were experimenting with pronouns and gender, but I never felt the need."

"Maybe I need to experiment too," I think out loud. "Try some names."

"Prudence."

"No!"

"Vincent."

"Hmmm."

"Oreo."

"What?"

"I'm hungry!" he laughs, and goes in search of snacks.

"I thought I understood things," I muse as he goes through the cupboards. "Maybe not everything, but most things. And me, I made sense. It sucks not to have that anymore. It fucking sucks."

Adam makes a listening sound, a deep hum like a far off cargo ship. He brings over a container of oatmeal raisin cookies and sets them on the counter. "It's a chance to find out who you are now, right? Not who you were, though I suppose that's a part of it. We change. We grow. That's what being alive is, isn't it? Can't stay in one spot forever."

I chew through a cookie, savouring the raisins. "You know what, yeah. Things make sense, but they don't really, 'cause you find out something, or part of it collapses. That's what this feels like. Trying to prop up something that's fallen apart."

"You don't look fallen apart to me," he says, and solemnly offers me another cookie.

CHAPTER TWENTY-SIX
Shady Hut

ACT LIKE EVERYTHING is normal, Jessica told me. So here I am, half-standing, half-sitting on a steel stool in the middle of the shopping centre selling sunglasses.

"Good morning!" I stand up to greet the potential customer.

The mall walker's jogging suit swishes as they power-walk past.

I sit back down. It'll be another fifteen minutes before they circle back to the other side of the sunglasses stand.

I type on the little desk attached to the *Shady Hut*, uploading the new ad to the slideshow cycling above the display racks. *Summertime can be all year long!* the laissez-faire font scrawls above a person wearing sunglasses. The figure's red and yellow swimsuit is bright against the backdrop of a frost-bitten cityscape.

"All year long!" I declare to the empty shopping centre.

Most of the stores are already open, but it'll be slow until 11, when Sunday breakfasts are over and people are getting out of religious services.

Reaching under the little desk, I take my phone from my jacket pocket. It's a newer model, but still one I could've had before…what happened. It strikes me that I haven't used it since meeting Jessica, only once to check the time. Weird. People are constantly on their phones, aren't they?

I press the home button twice to skip past the clock. The screen lights up, a blue background and no apps beyond the text and call icons. I go into the message field and open my contact list. There's only one number listed: "Home."

Someone wiped my phone. No friends, no lovers, no connections outside of what Marius needs me for. There's no way I would only use my phone to call home. What am I, 12 years old?

If I call 'Home,' who'll pick up?

"Excuse me."

There's a customer. Green hair hangs pin-straight from their angled, black beret. A cosmopolitan dress, cinched with a wide kaleidoscopic belt, hugs their tall frame. Tiny succulents cover their bare shoulders in patches of pistachio, light pink, and pale yellow.

I fumble my phone and try to hide it in my sweater pocket. "Um, yes, I work here, hello."

"Can I see those ones?" The customer points at a set of red-tinted lenses with thick white frames.

"Yeah, sure." I get up from the stool, slide sideways into the epicentre of the *Shady Hut*, where any wrong move results in stock collapse. I open the back of the display case and fish out the requested shades.

The customer tries them on. I hold up a round mirror as they find their best angle. Their pale face is striking, subtle blush on their prominent cheekbones, faint pink outlining their full lips. The eyes arcing over the sunglass rims are an ancient grey. "I'll take them."

"You'll have to pay for them first," I joke, opening a drawer and taking out a new case and a cleaning cloth.

The customer hands over a credit card, waving the extras away. "I'll wear them, from now on." I return their card, pass on their receipt.

"Thank you for shopping at the *Shady Hut*," I say as they crumple the receipt and shove it into the recesses of their handbag. "And have a wonderful—"

Suddenly, I wonder how long I've been working here, if this is another one of the lies Marcus planted in me.

The customer looks up from coaxing a turquoise succulent to lean away from their chin. *Yes?* their eyes seem to ask. The grey irises are tinted red, white sunglass frames circling them like smoke rings.

"A wonderful day, I mean."

"You too." They look at me a moment longer, then turn away. The succulents extend over their shoulders and meet at the nape of their neck, spanning their back like a plush pastel shawl.

The rest of the morning crawls by. No more customers. Most of the mall patrons are on their way to other places, other purchases.

Noon finally arrives and I lock the cases, pulling a cage cover over the advertising screen and the small desk. I'm just about to go on my mandated lunch break when I see her coming out of the bookstore down the hall. She walks through the now-populated thoroughfare, stopping on the other side of the *Shady Hut*, as if waiting for me.

"Hey Mom," I say, making a thing of placing the *Be Back Soon* sign on the display case. "Shopping?"

"You haven't been home much the past couple days." Her mouth presses in on itself, disapproving.

"Just hanging out with some friends."

"Oh? Anyone I know?"

"Just some friends, Mom." I have one arm in my coat, obviously glancing at the exit across from us.

"I wanted—" She takes a step closer. "I wanted to take you for lunch. If you're not busy."

I shrug, zipping up my coat even though the shopping centre is always a balmy 25 degrees Celsius.

Mom's matching green eyes glisten. "Oh, sweetheart. How did we get this way?"

"You tell me."

It's a novelty, being able to see over her head—most of my memories of her are from when I was much shorter. Across the walkway, kids kick their restless feet against the floor as they drink smoothies; a parent holds their child's hand; a swarm of teenagers buzzes into a tech shop.

We pick up some hamburgers from the food court and sit at one of the mushroom-style tables.

"So, what's this all about?"

Mom looks up from unwrapping her chicken burger-with-no mayo-no pickles. "Can't I take my kid for lunch?" She blinks innocently.

"They told you to check up on me, didn't they?"

"I don't know what you're talking about." Taking a bottle of strawberry-scented hand sanitizer from her purse, she administers some to her palms.

"Are you really my mom?"

She drops the bottle of hand sanitizer, her freed hand grabbing hold of mine, gripping it with a strength that makes me gasp. "How can you say that?" Her eyes brim over into full tears.

The fake strawberry smell is strong enough to make me gag, but I push through. "Listen, I know something's going on. I just want the truth for once. That's all I want."

She loosens her grip, and places her other hand on top of mine.

"You can nod, or laugh, whatever. Did they tell you to check up on me?"

Her hands press mine in confirmation.

"Are you my mom?"

A fierce, quick pressure.

"You're scared of them."

She laughs, a breathy giggle so far off from the full-body laugh that resonated through my childhood.

"You can tell them I've been at Jessica's. They're good people there, really. You don't have to worry."

Her hands let go and pluck a tissue from her purse. "But I do worry," she says, wiping beneath each eye in a slow arc. "What else is a parent supposed to do? Did I get it all?"

It takes me a second to realise she means her mascara. "Yeah, it barely ran. You're good."

"Oh, good." She sits back, stuffing the used tissue into her pocket. "Before I forget..." She digs deeper into her purse, pulling out a plastic bag, white and bulbous like a turnip. "I picked up something for you." She hands it to me, her voice nervous. "There's a receipt if you don't like it."

Inside the plastic bag is a long felt scarf, navy blue with grey snowflakes worked into the material. I wrap it three times around my neck, the tasselled ends resting against the front of my camouflage coat. "Thanks, Mom," I say, surprised that I mean it.

She smiles, a brief flash, before looking away. Her shoulders tense. "I might take a vacation soon, sweetheart. Somewhere warm."

"Sounds nice."

"But I wouldn't want to go if—"

"I'll be fine."

Her shoulders relax, and she lets out a small puff of air. "I didn't want to do it, but they made it very easy to see their point of view."

"What point of view is that?"

"Oh," she says, picking up her sandwich again, "You know."

"They're paying you to keep an eye on me. I wasn't living at home before any of this happened. I was living somewhere else when they took me. They changed things. But they needed somewhere familiar for me to stay, somewhere I wouldn't question. So they paid you to take me back and pretend as if everything was normal, like I never left—"

"Maybe that's the way it happened." She wipes the last spot of ketchup from the corner of her mouth. "Maybe I said yes because giving you a stable place was the only thing I could do for you. I don't know what all you're mixed up with, but I'm your parent. I'd rather you be at home with me than some cell somewhere, locked up until they needed you."

"Needed me for what?"

She stands up, her breathy laugh refusing to answer. "We should do this again!" she exclaims, bustling over to kiss my cheek. "I'll see you at home, call me if you'll be late getting in."

Before I can say goodbye, she walks out past the last cluster of tables and into the crowd heading for the exit. The mass of bodies swallows her up.

INTERLUDE THREE:
Reena's Sweet Sixteen

THE SPRING WATERS Retreat Centre was founded by Marya Haddad-Aguillard back in the '70s. Originally a one-room cabin, it was created as a direct response to the Neo-Essentialist ideology purported by the government regime of the time. "Birth Self, True Self" was the Neo-Essentialist party's motto. Parts swapping was outlawed, made out to be a sin by religious leaders; those who defied them were arrested or added to lists and denied healthcare, education, and marriage rights.

Those in power didn't follow their own rules, appearing as eternally youthful paragons of righteousness in the propaganda broadcasts, claiming their exceptional health was genetic. Gender was reduced to a binary based on a simplistic view of birth sex. Power, wealth, and virility were valued. The misfits, outliers, those in-between, were cast off, ridiculed, or worse. Spring Waters was a place for them to gather and fight for a more inclusive society. The Resistance March of '73, the key to the major government changeover in the following years, was planned at Spring Waters.

When Haddad-Aguillard retired from managing the retreat centre in '11, Lin took over. Xe expanded the single cabin layout to include dorms, a dining hall, and a workshop area for mutual aid groups. Although Neo-Essentialism had thankfully been whittled down to a small faction with no political power, the impact of the ideology remained. Even in a more tolerant society, people needed somewhere to actively work towards a hopeful future, individually and collectively.

In addition to all of this history, Spring Waters was also home to a runaway named Reena. She'd come to the retreat centre through the woods, dressed in a filthy sheet wrapped around tattered clothes and shoes. Lin stayed with her all through her recovery at the nearest hospital, and throughout the social services inquiry. Reena's ID chip was no help—it had been wiped, erasing the birth names of her parents and her family name. When no one stepped forward to claim Reena, Lin adopted her. After that, Reena lived at Spring Waters.

"You finished it!" Lin exclaimed as Reena came into xyr office. Xe set aside the half-filled-out grant application and spread xyr hands in appreciation of Reena's new sweater.

Reena stood very still in the middle of the room, wearing the red sweater she'd been crocheting for the past month. The sleeves were a little short, but she'd compensated by adding a black cuff. She studied it passively, then gave a small nod of her head. "It turned out more jolly than I intended."

Lin accepted the personification with a familiar shrug. "I think it looks great! So," xe smiled, "do you feel any older?"

"I guess."

"Sixteen's a big deal."

Giving another little nod, Reena sat in the padded spinning chair across from xem.

"Which is why…"

Reena glanced up quickly, knowing where this was going.

"…I got you something extra special."

Reena leaned forward a little, then sat back in the chair, trying not to seem too interested.

"Oh, enough with the detachment!" Lin poked fun, then revealed the wrapped rectangle from behind the desk. "Happy birthday!"

Reena received the gift, a gleam in her blue eyes. She unwrapped it carefully, pulling up the tape to preserve the wrapping paper. Inside was an envelope and a yellow hardback copy of the *Tao Te Ching*. She placed both on the desk.

"I know you wanted your own copy," Lin said as Reena held her emotions in check. "This is my favourite translation."

Reaching across the desk, Reena placed both her hands on Lin's. Reena didn't touch people on principle and Lin felt the significance of the moment. "Thank you," Reena said, and removed her hands. The moment passed, and Reena's expression shifted, her eyes flashing mischievously. "What if I don't show up for kitchen duty today?"

Lin laughed. "I already asked Javier to cover for you. But you have to show up to eat dinner, otherwise the rest of us will have to eat cake all by ourselves."

"Cake!" Reena exclaimed. "You weren't supposed to make a cake!"

"But it's fun!" Lin handed Reena the book and the envelope. "See you later?"

Reena nodded, joy radiating from her round, healthy face. Hugging the gift tightly to her chest, she strode out of the office.

Lin flipped through some forms on xyr desk, thinking over how far Reena had come in the past few years. After her recovery, she'd spent almost a year in silence. Lin had brought in counsellors, but Reena ignored their questions. The only thing she showed any interest in was learning. Learning how to sew, how to carve wood, how to make food into meals, learning how to read. There was no shortage of people coming through the retreat centre who had unique skills and were willing to share them with the quiet pre-teen.

When Reena refused to move away for junior high, Lin hired a tutor. Once she had a handle on reading, Reena devoured most of the books in the retreat centre's modest collection, many of them contemplative or activism-oriented. Reena avoided the overtly Christian books, leaning towards Taoist and Buddhist texts. Although Reena was serious as a rule, she'd started showing sparks of humour and mischief. Her health was good, she was bright and kind, and she thrived in her vibrant, ever-changing community. What more could you ask for a teenager?

Dinner that night was rambunctious, energy rushing between the Spring Waters staff and the retreaters, who could definitely tell that something special was going on. The meal was excellent, if eccentric, offering all of Reena's favourite foods in a buffet-style extravaganza of taste and colour: corn on the cob, enchiladas, vegetarian sushi, and broccoli with cheese sauce.

Only one person remained aloof from the celebratory atmosphere. A retreater, Allain, sat in front of the television which had been placed in the dining hall specifically so they could watch the evening news while they ate. It was a routine that they had indicated was important to them, and one which Spring Waters willingly accommodated.

During a lull in the dining hall conversation, the newscast informed the room that "...cult leaders have been apprehended after a stand-off at the church complex..."

Reena, who rarely watched TV, stood up from her half-finished plate and moved to stand beside Allain. Realising that something was wrong, Lin followed her. The three of them watched as the newscast rolled footage of officers breaking down a heavy wooden door to reveal a group of people huddled together—stained glass cast red and yellow and blue over their mouthless faces.

Reena let out a strangled cry and knelt in front of the TV. "The Mothers..." she whispered.

Upset by this interruption, Allain crossed their arms. Lin placed a hand on their shoulder, asking for patience.

One of the Mothers appeared on screen. Her mouth restored and her eyes wet with tears, she spoke into the reporter's microphone, pausing every couple of seconds to clear her throat. "We have been here for many years...we are glad...that we can leave...and...live freely."

The camera cut away to a different group of people who were being handcuffed and loaded into police vehicles.

Reena, who hadn't moved, now actively scanned their faces. "Where is he..." she muttered.

The footage of the church complex minimised to a square in the top corner, a news anchor appearing in the foreground. "....early reports have determined that Neo-Essentialism was the core of the organisation's ideology. The cult leaders have been apprehended and will await trial as the police continue the investigation…Back to you, Herb…"

Reena lowered her head, her hands gripping her knees.

"Hey," Lin said in a low voice, crouching down next to her. "What do you need?"

"The reporter said that the cult leaders have been apprehended?"

"Yes."

"All of them?"

"I don't know, Reena."

"I didn't see him."

"Who?"

"The Father. I didn't see him. But they said the cult leaders have been apprehended…" Reena pushed away from the screen and grabbed Lin's hand for the second time in one day. This time, her grip would have broken a pencil in half. "Tell me they arrested him."

"Come on," Lin said gently, leading her away from the television. "Let's go to my office and we can talk about it."

Reena startled everyone by bursting into tears.

#

Reena told Lin everything. The cult. The Mothers. The rows of mouths imprisoned in glass jars.

"I failed them," Reena said after a long silence. "I left them there to suffer."

"No," Lin said. "You were a child when you escaped, and very scared. That's why you never said anything. You thought you'd be sent back there."

"But I learned that wouldn't happen. Why didn't I speak up then?"

Lin crossed xyr hands on the desk and took a deep breath. "Would you like to now?"

Uncertainty flitted across Reena's face. "Would it help?"

"Who knows," Lin said truthfully, "but it would help you, if nothing else."

"The Mothers are the ones who matter," Reena said forcefully. "I'll do it."

Lin called the sheriff's office in the nearby town and arranged an interview for the following day.

Reena gave her statement, but was never called on to appear in court. Lin suggested she start counselling sessions, which she stuck with for a few months, before expressing her preference for meditation. Reena sought out quiet places and quiet people and never spoke of her experiences with the cult again.

As summer was nearing its end, Reena knocked on Lin's office door.

"Come on in!" Feet crossed on the desk, Lin reclined in the padded rolling chair, watching the hanging spider plant spin slowly in the breeze from the open windows. "I was thinking about making some tea.. .Oh, Reena," Lin moved xyr feet off the desk.

Ever since her birthday and the news broadcast, Reena had worn simple grey clothing; the bright red sweater and the mischievous gleam in her eyes had been put away somewhere.

"Is green tea okay?" Lin was aware of trying to keep a tender note out of xyr voice. In spite of everything she'd been through, in spite of everything Lin knew, Reena needed normalcy most of all.

"Yes."

Lin busied xemself with the office kettle, setting each of them up with a mug of hot tea before returning to xyr chair.

Cross-legged on the low pouffe seat, Reena stared into her mug.

"How are you doing?" Lin asked in the most normal way possible.

Reena set her tea on the floor. "I wanted to ask you something."

"Okay," Lin said, bracing for things teenagers usually ask for. Maybe a cell phone or a bigger room or—

"Can I...leave?"

Completely sidelined, Lin closed xyr eyes. "Leave?" Xe tried to figure out where this was coming from. Settling on an option, Lin met Reena's steady blue gaze. "You can leave anytime, you know that. Is there something in town you need? Or," and Lin felt a drop in xyr stomach, "are you thinking about high school? We can find a place close by, or there are schools with dorms we can check out—"

"That's not what I mean," Reena interrupted gently. "I mean..." She hesitated, as if unsure of how to put her feelings into words. "I think it's time for me to go somewhere, try something new. I'm sixteen now, and...I like it here. But I need to do something. Out there."

"What kind of something?" Lin relaxed. Xe recognized the feeling of restlessness that had afflicted xem as a teenager.

"Something that helps people, and somewhere far away." Reena lowered her gaze. "It's too close here, sometimes."

Lin guessed that she meant the cult, her past. "I understand."

Having asked what she came to ask, Reena picked up her tea and sipped at it. "Is that okay?"

Lin nodded through a sip of tea, through xyr proud tears. "I have someone in mind. She lives in a big city. I think you'd be a big help to the work she does there. But if you don't like it, you can come home, no questions asked."

"I'm ready," Reena said, resolute.

"Yes," Lin replied. "I know you are."

CHAPTER TWENTY-SEVEN
Nice Running Into You

AFTER WORK, I head down to the riverfront and find a bench to wait out the rest of the day. It's cold enough that I bury my face in my new scarf, cup my hands around the coffee I picked up on my way out of the shopping centre. Seven hours, and only three pairs of sunglasses sold. Makes me want to weep.

I should quit, I tell myself as sluggish ice floes collide in the narrow strip of river. The sunglasses job is part of Marius's plan, whatever that was. But I'm okay now. I changed my hand, got that fucking nightmare out of my brain.

What was it for? an inner voice whispers. *Don't you want to know?*

The day after my check-in at the hospital, I went to the police station. Even though Jessica showed them the device from inside my head and I told them everything I could remember, the officer interviewing me didn't seem in much of a hurry to follow up on it.

"You'll hear from us if we have any more questions," they said, casually leaning an arm on the doorframe to the back offices. "Nothing we can do right now."

"What do you mean there's nothing you can do?" Jessica growled. "Marius is behind it, why don't you investigate?"

The officer shrugged. "No motive. What makes you so sure blondie here wasn't being paid to try out new equipment?"

"Tampering with a person's brain is illegal!" Jessica shouted. "It's a crime, which is what you officers are supposed to be preventing!"

"Hey, don't get all hysterical—"

Jessica wheeled away from the officer, her trench coat flapping madly around her as she stormed out of the office. "No good," she seethed as we crossed the foyer. "They won't touch Marius."

I shiver from the memory, crossing my arms. My breath goes up in a wall of fog. Should've hung around the mall after work, where it was warm and full of people.

I dig the cell phone out of my coat pocket. It's a pretty nice model—sleek black finish, a multi-lensed front camera. Empty. One number saved in the contacts. No one to call. I set it on the bench and sip on the tepid coffee.

Someone appears on the river path leading from downtown. They're tall, walking with long easy strides as if the cold doesn't bother them. A three-quarter length tweed coat hangs open over a faded hoodie, tan pants tucked into red winter boots topped with sheep wool—

"Adam!" I wave.

He angles my way, skirting a pile of snow. "Hi!" He stops in front of me, his usually tired eyes shining with energy. "How's today going?"

"Keeping it ordinary," I smile. "But I might have to quit my job. It's boring as hell."

Adam laughs, kicking at a chunk of ice. "Then I support your decision."

"Thanks. Where're you off to?"

"The train station."

"Going on a trip?"

"Reena's due back any time now. Mom's borrowing the Jeep, but I thought why not walk there, get some exercise?"

"Reena." My stomach drops. "Right, I totally forgot."

"You should come!"

"That's probably not a good idea."

"Why not?"

I shrink inside my jacket. "She hates me."

"What?" Adam's eyebrows shoot up. "You're not serious."

"The way she looks at me? Definitely some bad vibes there."

"That…" his expression folds in on itself as he searches for an explanation. "Maybe she doesn't know you feel that way."

"Oh, she knows." I think back to the day we first met, her blue-eyed scowl. Of course, she knows.

"You should come," Adam says, thoughtful. "A lot's happened since she left, maybe we can help each other understand what's going on."

I consider this for a minute. I could stay on this bench until I get too cold and go home to have more cryptic conversations with Mom. Or, I could take a 20-minute walk to the train station alone with Adam.

"Alright, I'll tag along." I get up and stamp my feet a couple of times on the concrete.

As we move away, I glance over my shoulder at the empty cell phone on the bench—and leave it behind.

Swallowing a cold sip, I bare my teeth, the taste of bad coffee coating my mouth. "I have to stop drinking this."

"Here," Adam takes the mostly empty paper cup from me and runs up the path to a garbage bin.

Surprised, I laugh, the warmth of it filling my cheeks.

We continue past a section of riverfront housing and a row of apartments peeking over the top of a white hill. The river path curves to follow the water.

"That's what Reena says," Adam speaks into the comfortable quiet. "Water always runs downhill; we should be like water and seek out the lowest places."

"What does that even mean?" I laugh, unkindly this time.

"Don't chase after the high things—fame, money, what society values. Seek out the people society says are lowest—the poor, the sick, the mistreated. Acknowledge the low parts of yourself, and let the water flow through them, making them places of life and fulfilment."

"I'm not really into religion," I say, a little bewildered at his train of thought.

"Sorry, the river just reminded me of it." His face radiates contentment—his cheeks would be flushed, if they could be. Maybe it's the brisk walk. Maybe it's something else.

I don't want to believe it, but I decide to sound him out anyway. "Hey, so—you and Reena are pretty close? Jessica was telling me."

"Oh, the fever-of-105 story?" He stuffs his hands in his pockets. "She likes to tell that one, it's a crowd-pleaser."

"Do you, I mean…do you like Reena?"

"Of course I do," Adam says cheerfully through his wounded expression.

His answer puts a lump in my stomach. How could anyone *like* Reena?

The sun starts to set downstream; the thin, winter air takes on a yellow hue. Our shadows are distinct, life-sized cut-outs on the snow.

The path splits and we take the branch angling up towards the street. Scattered salt crunches under our shoes—melted snow seeps all the way through to my socks. The wind picks up as we climb higher, sieving through the back of my coat.

Crossing the main road, we pass the distillery district and finally make it to the train station. A low, unimpressive building with a corrugated tin roof sits on the platform.

The sliding door stutters open. The floor is covered in brown and light blue tiles. A ticket desk overlooks the rows of joined bucket seats facing the floor-to-ceiling window next to the arrivals gate.

Adam sits in the row closest to the window and stretches his thin arms overhead. "5:03," he consults the analog clock hanging over the ticket booth. "Almost time."

I hesitate, then sit firmly in the seat next to him, warming my hands under my thighs.

"We beat Jessica here?"

We crane our heads over the back of our seats, scan the room, but there's only a handful of people scattered between the vending machine and the map rack. Definitely no Jessica.

"How's your recovery going, by the way?" Adam asks.

"Memory's still patchy." I think through all of the images I've gathered over the past few days. Most of the ones from the past two years are unmoored, snapshots of nameless faces or snippets of conversation. But there's one thing that almost feels right. "I think I'm going to stick with Nan. At least for now."

"Nan-for-Now." Adam smiles. "It suits you."

The way he says it makes me feel very okay to be Nan-for-Now.

A train slides along the platform and slows to a stop. Adam's colourless eyes fix on the window.

Passengers make the big step down from the train to the platform, pillows under arms, backpacks slung over half-open coats. I have to comb through all of the people getting off the train twice before I recognise her.

Recognise is the wrong word. As the person wearing a grey winter coat crosses the platform, I clock the blue eyes, the pouting mouth, but something is very different. Even when she comes into the station, her breath disappearing in the warmth, her face puffy and haggard, I don't recognise her. Something is very wrong.

She's momentarily swallowed by the crowd pushing through the gate. When the strangers clear away, Reena is left standing with a cloth suitcase in one hand, her hair curling over her forehead down over her eyebrows. When she spots Adam, her round shoulders and travel-weary face relax.

That's what's missing. The hostile vibe usually hanging over Reena is totally gone, as if a blackout curtain has been pulled aside, revealing a clear, night sky beyond.

She notices me. I expect her to glower, make some passive aggressive comment. Instead, she nods, her blue eyes curious instead of cold.

Jessica arrives, her sharp profile displaying concern mingled with relief. Adam waves to me, and I follow them out of the train station, navigating around families reuniting, people on their phones, the epic line up for the bathroom.

Cold touches my face. I watch as Reena tosses her suitcase through the hatch in the back of the Jeep. Adam offers her the front, even though his legs will be cramped sitting behind her. Jessica opens the driver's side door, her free hand making a wide sweeping gesture as Reena steps up into the passenger's side.

I slink into the seat behind Jessica, my insides feeling out of place. My long-dormant exit light flickers in the dark.

As Jessica starts the car, Reena angles her face towards me. "Still with us?" she asks, her blue eyes steady, her tone almost teasing.

Blindsided, I nod. Something is definitely wrong. Reena would never talk to me like that before she left. I study her in the rearview mirror as the Jeep turns onto the main highway. Her pouting mouth that never smiles, that hasn't changed. Her eyes, that's where the difference is. No judgemental looks, no ice-shard glares. It's as if—

"Stop the car!" I yell through the panicked fist pushing up my throat.

Jessica checks the mirrors and cranks the wheel, coming to a halt on the gravel shoulder. I clip open the door, miss the step down, and stumble towards the dead grass and gravel-pocked slush lining the road.

The epiphany fills me as my eyes pick out a dried thistle in the stalks. I was wearing glasses before, dread-tinted lenses that made Reena seem like a threat. And now that the glasses are off—

The fist pushes up my throat, and I let it, gagging as watery brown vomit spatters the grass.

Jessica is beside me, rubbing my back in slow waves, like Adam did in the alley.

"I think," I say to Jessica's dark waiting eyes, "I think I need to talk to Mr. Snaff."

CHAPTER TWENTY-EIGHT
Grit Your Teeth

"COME IN, MY dears, come in!"

Mr. Snaff opens the door wide, and we pile into the narrow boot room. The shelves lining the walls overflow with shoes.

"There are hooks for your coats, but leave your shoes on, of course! All shoes are welcome in my home!" He smiles widely at us.

Once we've hung up our coats, he leads us through a glass-panelled door into a modest living room. A desk in the corner is piled high with stacks of papers, used tea cups, wire canisters crammed with pens and screwdrivers of all sizes, and an open laptop. An old radio case balances precariously on a tower of math textbooks.

"Such a mess!" he chuckles. "I asked Miles to clean up his toys before he left, but I didn't follow through with my own! The hypocrisy of parenthood!"

Jessica settles on a plush orange ottoman. "I was hoping to see him while we were here."

"Holland took him to soccer practice, and for ice cream after, I expect!" Mr. Snaff smiles widely again and takes a velcro wallet from the back pocket of his dress pants. "I still like a printed out copy," he hands me the wallet. "It's nice to have them on my phone of course, but I'm old fashioned that way!"

Inside is a photo of Mr. Snaff with his arm around a person in a tweed suit who I assume is Holland. Between them is a kid around ten years old, holding up a trophy.

"The year Miles won the city-wide spelling bee!" Mr. Snaff exclaims proudly as I return the wallet to him. "He's a very bright child. Holland and I are extremely proud of him."

"He's going to be twelve soon," Jessica sighs. "They grow up faster than we'd like, don't they?"

"Oh yes!" Mr. Snaff bends his whole torso in agreement. "I still remember the day he was born. I was in labour for 36 hours, and when he came out screaming, it was the most blessed sound I'd ever heard in my life. Always a vocal child! Once he learned a few words, well, then he started making sentences and the rest, as they say, is history!" Mr. Snaff's already tilted back-eyes look thoughtfully at the ceiling. "Always wanted to try for another one..."

"You still can," Jessica offers.

Mr. Snaff twists his torso back and forth. "One is blessing enough. Besides, I have all of my students to worry about! What a rambunctious group this year! But here I am, rambling on. You said on the phone that our friend here has a question for me?" Mr. Snaff rolls the desk chair next to the couch and relaxes into it.

"That thing in my head," I say, tasting the bile still coating the inside of my mouth. "Do you think it could've changed the way I see certain things, certain people?"

Mr. Snaff hums. "It's possible. Although the equipment itself was straightforward, the program could've been extremely complex. There were communication points with various areas of your brain...But before I resort to conjecture, tell me more about what you experienced. What kinds of things look different to you now?"

"Reena," I say, nervously.

Reena remains curious, all sense of foreboding gone.

"When we first met, I was afraid of you. You would give me awful looks and you said strange things, like you were threatening me somehow."

Her face tightens with confusion. "I never meant...Sometimes it's difficult...putting my thoughts into words. I'm sorry if I said anything that made you feel uncomfortable."

If I'm right, she has nothing to be sorry about. "When I brought it up earlier today, Adam didn't know what I was talking about, and when I saw you at the train station—" I swallow. "You seemed so approachable, so non-threatening, so different from everything I thought you were. I think—I think the program or whatever, was trying to make you seem like someone who couldn't be trusted. Even a threat. And I'm scared because I know that my old hand was programmed for violence..." I look at my hands, the tan right hand resting over the left. "What if Marius wanted me to kill you?"

Mr. Snaff gets up from his chair. Muttering, he sifts through a sleeve of papers on the desk. "I drew a rough diagram of how the contraption was set up, for reference." He frees a sheet, pointing at the outline of what looks like a circuit. "Simply put, there was a node at your visual centre, which may have gathered stimuli and fed it back to your interpretation centre with small adjustments. That would have to be a sophisticated system. But if it was just one person the program was targeting—it's very possible."

Adam's brow bunches up, his voice crackling with urgency. "Why would Marius want to kill Reena? What reason could he possibly have? The lawsuit from five years ago? Mom?"

Jessica punches down on a couch pillow. "But what about the fingers? Marius said that Reena would understand."

Reena cuts herself off from the conversation—arms and legs crossed, her eyes closed.

"Reena?" Jessica reaches over and places a hand on her knee.

In the tense silence, I find myself looking at a model plane hanging from a low part in the ceiling. It's painted a mustard yellow, the front propeller covered in rust, the double-decker wings held apart with toothpicks.

"I don't want to go into it," Reena says, her pout pronounced, her words serious and low. "But Marius is working for someone, maybe a group of people, I'm not sure. And I think they would kill me, if they could."

Drugs is my guess. Maybe Reena used to be involved somehow, pissed off the wrong people or didn't pay. It doesn't seem to fit, but people are unpredictable. They have pasts. So drugs, probably. What else could it be?

"We could go to the police?" Adam says, already expecting Jessica's answer.

"Marius bought them off," Jessica growls. Her eyes scan the room as if for a way out.

"But Mr. Snaff removed the program," I say, hopeful. "That means when they try to activate it, it fails, right?"

Mr. Snaff rocks his body from side to side, thoughtfully. "There may be some residual impact," his eyes crinkle in triumph, "but you're correct. With the program and apparatus removed, you should be able to recognize any implanted promptings and resist them!"

"Doesn't matter," Reena says, still as a stone. "They know where I am. And there's still one finger to be delivered."

Adam stands up. "Let's go. Right now. I know a ton of places, safe places."

She runs a hand up her forehead, holding the hair away from her eyes. "Doesn't matter," she says. "I'll meet whatever comes."

"Don't apply the Dao to this Reena! This is your life, not a philosophical discussion!"

"What's the difference?" She un-stones herself, unfolding her limbs until she is once again just a human sitting on the edge of the couch.

CHAPTER TWENTY-NINE
Slip Through Your Fingers

JESSICA DROPS US off at the apartment and pulls away to return the Jeep. Reena goes first up the fire escape, her cloth suitcase hefted in one hand. As she unlocks the door, I realise Adam isn't following; he stands in the alley, hands in his tweed pockets.

"See you later," he mumbles, and strides further down the sidewalk.

We go in, Reena moving ahead in the dark, flipping light switches. The bare front room, the wall of paintings, the rug and chair set by the patio door snap out of darkness, like pictures in a pop-up book.

"Make yourself at home," Reena says on her way to the hall. Her bedroom door shuts gently behind her.

I fill a glass of water at the kitchen tap and swirl the last of the vomit taste from behind my teeth, spit it down the drain. I gulp the rest of the water down, and set the glass on the counter.

A small shadow curls around my leg. I look down in surprise, but it's only No Name, left alone all day in an empty apartment, hungry for affection.

Wind rips around the building, banging at the walls and rattling the old kitchen window. I stretch out on the rug by the patio door, which looks newer and is properly sealed, soundproof. Snow swirls through the streetlight glow. A newspaper hanglides up from the gutter. The boulevard trees brandish their bare branches. Inside, it's perfectly still.

No Name curls at my elbow. I shift onto my side so I can scratch around his ears.

Reena's door opens and she comes out of the hallway, carrying a yellow, hardcover book. Her hair is cut short again. She sits on the rug, facing me.

"Aren't you afraid?" I ask.

No Name stretches and stalks over to press against Reena's knee. She rubs her fingers together, an invitation. He jumps up into her lap.

"Living, dying. Doesn't matter. All part of the flow of the universe."

"Adam clearly disagrees." I sit up. "I think it matters to him very much whether you live or die."

She looks out the patio door, stroking No Name's back. "Hold onto things too tightly, and they slip through your fingers."

"So you're not even going to try and get away? You're going to just let them kill you?"

"I never said that." She raises her eyebrows, a mysterious expression on her lips. "Do without doing. Seems like apathy, but it's wise. It's like water, letting gravity take it to the lowest point, yet carving the landscape as it goes. It does without doing because of what it is."

"All this religious shit is beyond me." I pull my knees to my chest.

"Not religion," she replies. "A way of looking at things."

"Right."

No Name purrs. Reena's massive hand rests on his side, protective. "I tried hiding. Tried running. So now, I have to follow where the river carves. That being said," she sighs. "I am afraid." Heavy eyelids obscure her blue eyes as her full-moon face angles into shadow.

CHAPTER THIRTY
Silver Spoon

AMBER WALKS UP the marble stairway, marveling at the opulent porch extending from either side. Ceramic mosaics of birds and flowers cover the floor. Pure white, wicker furniture lounges around glass tables as tall heat lamps keep away the chill.

She reaches the front door, a glossy wooden panel twice as big as a regular entryway, and presses the doorbell set in the frame. Her third eye notices a small statue in the garden bed—a figure in a ripped dress transforming into a tree as another figure in fancy clothing reaches after them. Amber glances at the fountain beside it, out of order for the season, the stone bowl lined with snow.

She rings the bell again. A person wearing a black suit opens the door, welcoming her inside. "Please, let me take your jacket."

She hurries to remove her coat, uneasy under their intense stare. The way their pupils focus on her yet beyond her—the parts are tech. It makes her uncomfortable, thinking about what information they could be pulling up.

"This way."

She follows them across a richly-carpeted entryway. A round pedestal in the centre of the vaulted area features a statuette of a swan proudly extending its neck, wings arching in preparation for flight.

The person in the black suit leads her into a sitting room with a window overlooking the back of the house. The view is bleak: snow covers a flat plain of land that goes on for an acre until an iron fence rears to contain it. It reminds her of the frozen lake behind Spring Waters, and Reena's warning.

"He only uses the feminine," she whispers, before shaking it from her mind.

"Tea?" The person in the black suit turns from a stocked side table.

"No, thanks." Amber takes a breath, forcing her nervous legs to relax.

"Shouldn't be too long of a wait," they say, closing the door behind them.

Why did Marius invite me over? Amber wonders, crossing her legs and crimping the hem of her black dress in her hands. *Did I mess up that badly?*

No, a voice inside her soothes, *you did well, he wants to congratulate you, welcome you into the inner circle of the business. This is the chance you've been waiting for. Do you want to be a sales clerk for the rest of your life, selling other people the hands that should be yours? Don't mess this up, and you'll be set.*

Right, she straightens her back, *this is what I've been working towards.* She stands up and moves to a painting mounted on the wall. She studies it with practiced attention, waiting for Marius to come in so she can turn winningly toward him, as if startled out of a pleasant daydream.

But time passes and he doesn't come.

She doesn't see much in the painting anyway, so she wanders over to the tea table. There's a glass kettle filled with water. She clicks it on, watching the water temper slowly into bubbles, a raging roil that the system subdues with a click of the mechanism. She selects rosehip tea from a labelled canister, places the bag in the bottom of a gold-rimmed cup, and pours scalding water until it is submerged, drowning in its own rose-scented essence. She finds a silver spoon set, ready, in the sugar bowl, and adds a sliver of crystals to the tea. She's started counting calories again, but a little sugar won't hurt. She stirs it in, leaves the utensil and the soggy tea bag on a porcelain plate.

Perched on the white leather chair, Amber blows across the tea cup, holding it delicately and waiting for Marius to open the door.

He doesn't come.

Her tea gets cool enough to drink. She sets it on the table and readjusts her skirt over her thighs. Her third eye blinks dreamily. If Marius doesn't come soon, she's going to have to apologise to the person in the black suit on her way out. She's supposed to meet Cam for dinner.

Fuck Cam, the voice starts up again, its brazenness giving her a shiver of pleasure. *You're here to forward your career, to take your place behind the scenes, get a real share of the business.*

Right, she gives the door a determined glare. *Just let them try to take me out of here before Marius arrives.*

She reaches for her drink and takes a small sip. The tea is strong, the sugar just enough to make it drinkable. She drains the rest of the lukewarm tea and sets the cup down.

As she stares out the window, strange things begin to happen. The sun drops behind the iron fence. The items with her in the room stretch into impossible sizes while she shrinks, at the bottom of a well, power cables clamped to bolts sticking out from her temples.

Voices echo around her in the darkness.

"...not enough time for a full programming," Marius's voice surfaces through the cacophony. "...the other one is compromised...damn bleeding hearts..."

Another familiar voice responds, but she can't quite place it. "...we only need this one for the final...keep her close until then...any more mistakes, and I will take it personally..."

Who is it? she strives through the darkness, trying to place the familiar voice.

A massive shock jolts through her body. Her third eye rolls back in her head as Marius speaks directly into her ear:

"Listen to him... *absolute ... in the side...in the side...*"

A commanding face, frightening in its perfect symmetry, glares down at her—

Amber wakes up in the sitting room. The window is dark and a small lamp casts a weak circle of light over her empty tea cup.

A quiet knock at the door. Marius comes in, his expression apologetic. "I didn't want to wake you," he says, "but Cameron's been calling, wondering where you are."

"Oh my god!" Amber sits up, brushing a stray hair back from her eyes. "I'm so sorry, I don't—How long have I been asleep?"

"A couple of hours." Marius settles onto a settee.

"I am *so* sorry," she says again, inwardly screaming. "What did you want to discuss?"

Marius holds up a hand. "I've asked a lot of you the past couple of weeks, Amber. I truly appreciate all that you do for *High Five*. I see potential there. Potential that the company could benefit from. But unfortunately," he looks at his watch, a silver face embedded in his wrist, "I can't discuss the details with you right now, as I have a plane to catch."

Amber inhales sharply, using all of her willpower to keep herself from jumping with glee. "You mean..."

"Yes, Amber," he stands, his hand extended. "I have a contract all drawn up for your new position."

"Thank you!" Amber exclaims, propelling herself out of the chair and shaking his hand. "Thank you so much."

Marius leads her out of the room, a hand on her elbow. "I won't be back in town until next week," he speaks into her ear, "but when I return, we'll go for dinner to seal the deal."

Amber grins at him, and loses her balance. "Oh, clumsy me," she giggles. "I guess I'm not awake yet."

Marius's hand steadies her. "Until next week, then." He smiles, close-lipped.

The person in the black suit materialises from the shadows near the front door. They help Amber put on her coat and support her as she half-stumbles down the stairs. They put her into the back of a long white car.

Amber rests her face against the cool, leather seat as the hum of wheels beneath her crescendos to a roar.

CHAPTER THIRTY-ONE
Adrenaline Rush

IT'S BEEN A few days since I've been back at the *Beauty Mark*, but for the sake of keeping up appearances, I figure I should go. The bouncer is new, a football-player type in a gold and black turtleneck, their hair platinum spikes. They wave me through with barely a glance at my ID.

Nothing's changed inside, it never does. Bass shakes the floor and the communal mass of dancing bodies move in unison. The bartender is the same— they look up and recognise me. "Whatcha having?"

"Rum and coke, please!" I yell across the counter and pull up a bar stool.

I scan the room for sunglasses or a third eye, but Marius and the *High Five* clerk don't seem to be around.

The bartender sets my drink on the counter and I hand them a ten, shaking my head as they offer to return with change. I remember coming here after meeting the Fits. This bartender warned me about Marius. They're not on his side.

The drink fizzes in my mouth. I try to make it last, taking small sips of the caramel liquid. Funny to think that they used to pour coke on roads to get the bloodstains out. The thought finds its way to my stomach, carbonation scouring my insides.

Even though the *Beauty Mark* is probably another memory-plant, I don't mind it. It helps, the noise pressing on my ears, the people moving around me, the social economy of a bar that's easy to understand.

My attention wanders to the only other person sitting at the bartop. They're stocky, with a broad face, their fitted, denim vest showing off thick upper arms. They wear high-waisted cargo pants and flat galoshes. Wild blue hair.

The person from the Polaroid.

They sit with their back to the bar, leaning on their elbows. Mismatched hands hang lazily from their wrists. One hand is olive-toned, an original, with nails painted electric blue to match their hair. The other hand is a few shades lighter with tattoos stacked up between their knuckles. They glance behind them for the bartender, and catch me staring.

"What?" their posture asks through the music thrumming from the dance floor.

I direct my eyes down to the watermarked marble counter, then up again. The familiarity of their presence tugs at me. They seem to sense it as well, their brown eyes widening slightly. Their tattooed hand waves me over.

I drain my rum and coke, slide off the bar stool. Passing a half-dozen seats, I settle on the one next to them.

"It's been awhile." Their voice has a low timbre that stirs something deep inside me. "You changed your face."

"I'm sorry," I flip through my limited stack of memories. "I...know you. I just don't remember—"

"I haven't changed that much!" they exclaim. "Just got this piece to wear when I'm not at work." They hold up their tattooed hand between us.

"But seriously, nothing?" Their vibrant eyes glance over my face, catch on my mismatched hands. "You're going to have to start from the beginning. I can't believe you would leave for six months without telling me and then show up totally made over."

"I don't think I can. Start from the beginning, that is."

"Start in the middle then."

"What's your name?"

"Still Yarro."

"Yarro," I feel the name in my mouth. "Six months?"

"Yeah. You'd been talking about college for a while. When you stopped answering my texts...I guess I just assumed you went, since I never heard from you after that." Yarro leans back on the bar again, their face turned fully to mine, a challenge. "Wasn't fair."

And I can hear that voice again, in the depths of my memory—a voice low with longing, the blinds closed against the daylight, a lonely tang in my gut.

"What was I like back then?" I ask, an apology.

Yarro's eyes widen with surprise. "Two more over here!" they yell across the counter.

The bartender's hands are pale white, the stouts they set down rich loam, an inch of foam swaying up to the glass rims.

Yarro picks up their drink. We cheers, mirthless.

"This place is an antique, but I like it once in a while." Yarro runs their tongue quickly over their lips, clearing the ivory foam.

I shrug and take a tentative sip of my own beer. It's heavy like mercury, dark like the bottom of the sea. Yeasty, not bitter, but strong. Iron-hearted.

"The beer's good, at least."

I can sense their discomfort, as thick as the taste of beer in my mouth. "I honestly don't remember," I say, "but I don't think I meant to leave, I—"

Can I trust them, says something in my brain, *can I trust—*

"I'm going by Nan for now."

"Nan, okay." Their blue hair glows in the dim light. "So you've got amnesia."

"Guess so."

What else would I call it?

Yarro's lips shift into a lopsided grin, toothy and wicked in a way that opens up my lungs and makes me dizzy with oxygen. "Wanna do something crazy?"

#

Yarro's dressed for the weather in a black down-filled jacket, fake fur rimming the cuffs. They lead the way down the sidewalk, breaking the gale that tugs at the top of my hood. A whip-flash of wind curves around them, freezing my bare fingers holding the scarf up around my face. We don't even try to talk through the cold.

Crossing an empty street, we descend a short staircase into a covered entryway. Old leaves cake the corners, clumps of snow litter the concrete, an empty water bottle and a greasy sandwich bag huddle around the drain.

Yarro knocks on the reinforced window in the middle of the steel door.

A brief wait.

A high-pitched creak as the door swings open.

A thin Black guy in a loose tank top, his shoulder-length braids tied back with a floral scarf, quickly waves us inside.

"Christ, Yarro, it's late," he yawns.

It's not a room we're in, more of a hallway, with a closed door on either side. There's a worse-for-wear plastic chair next to the door and a small table stacked with unopened mail.

The guy who lives here presses his palms against his eyes and shakes his head a little. He blinks, staring at me with recognition. "*L'errant revient!* Long time no see!" He pulls me into a friendly hug.

"Hey, Sid," Yarro says, "give them some space, okay?"

"Oooh, *jalouse!*" Pulling back, Sid holds me by the shoulders. His chin and cheekbones peak like mountains, his gold eyes as calm as sunset lakes. Sid looks me over like a kid reacquainting themselves with a friend after summer vacation. "Love what you've done with the place. You've got some explaining to do—Yarro's been worried sick!"

Yarro rolls their eyes. "Come on, let them introduce themself."

Sid releases my shoulders and puts his hands on his hips. "Well?"

I wave, suddenly shy. "I'm Nan."

"New digs, new name, I like it." Sid gently punches my arm and turns to Yarro. "I get the feeling that something else is going on here. Nan's being awfully coy."

Yarro's eyes roll the whole of their compass. "Do you still have those cafeteria trays?"

"Cafeteria—oh, you mean the metal trays from the catering job?"

"Yeah, can I borrow one?"

"I mean sure, but—"

"Now, please."

Sid shrugs and goes into the room next to the unopened mail.

"I know him?" I ask Yarro in a half-whisper.

"He's being such an asshole," Yarro says, but doesn't answer my question.

Sid reappears in the doorway carrying a scratched-to-shit steel tray.

Yarro takes it without a word.

Unfazed, Sid turns a smile to me. "You take care, Nan." Sid holds up a palm for a high five then opens the door with a grand sweep of his arm.

"See y'all." He winks at Yarro and quickly shuts the door before they can respond.

Stomping up the stairs, Yarro makes an exasperated *arg* in their throat.

I follow them up the cold concrete back onto the sidewalk. "You okay?"

"Sid's *such* an asshole! I thought he'd be cool about you being back, but he just—*arg*!"

The street is clear of cars. The wind settles down. We walk in silence.

"Why do you think people use body parts as insults?" Yarro asks suddenly, their breath misting over the collar of their jacket.

"Like asshole? I don't know. Relatable, I guess."

"Yeah, everyone's got an asshole. Those Essentialist-nazis had it all wrong: there's nothing better or worse about having certain parts. Nothing wrong with changing yourself to reflect who you are. Nothing wrong with loving your body for what it is, for what it can do. Like, all of it's holy, all of it's good."

"Everything is holy. Every asshole," I smile. "Even Sid."

"He's a holy fucking asshole."

We both laugh.

Yarro's a head taller than I am, their blue hair tinged red under the streetlights. Our laughter runs out. The hum of a truck rumbles down a distant street.

"Where are we going?" I ask as Yarro strikes out from the sidewalk towards a dark patch of trees.

"I told you," they grin, pulling at my hand. "We're going to do something crazy."

I should be nervous, I think. Maybe this is where Marius gets me, with some made-up past. But I know that Yarro isn't fake. We recognised each other, not a planted memory. Intuition. The sense that lives in the body, that fills the mind with knowing. Gentle as a fragrance in the air.

We cross the treeline, a packed-down ribbon of path rolling out ahead of us. Yarro takes us a few metres in before crossing a small clearing in the stick trees.

The snow here's up past my ankles, no heat from the street, no constant passing of feet and tires wearing the snow into grey slush. My toes start to go numb.

Dropping down into a hollow, we reach what looks like an electrical station. A concrete platform sits at the top of a clear slope, the snow pristine and bright. It's completely quiet, trees providing cover from the wind.

"Okay, ready?" Yarro steps onto the platform. A concrete bannister runs from the edge down into the snow. Water that melted off the roof of the electrical building has frozen over the platform and the bannister in long twisted tendrils of ice.

Yarro sets the cafeteria tray on the top of the wide bannister, testing it, putting half their weight forward then settling back, readjusting. They cross their arms, hit the opposite shoulders and shout "ha!"

Jumping onto the metal tray, they slide down the icy bannister and onto the slope. The tray glosses over the snow as momentum carries them down the hill until Yarro loses their balance and rolls the last few metres to the bottom.

The rich sound of Yarro's laughter echoes through the trees. They trudge back up the hill, hair damp at the ends, clumps of snow sticking to the cuffs of their jacket.

"So, what do you think?" Yarro asks as they reach me with a grin as brilliant as a half moon.

"That was pretty crazy," I laugh.

Yarro holds out the christened metal tray. "Your turn."

The steel is cold on my fingers. The ice-covered platform and bannister, the three foot drop to the ground, and the slope hedged in by dense walls of black trees put a pit in my stomach. "I'll just watch."

"Come on, you got this." They tug me over to the platform.

I mount the short staircase, my soles barely getting traction on the ice.

"Okay, you don't want to rush it, but don't sit too long, otherwise you'll freeze."

"Literally or mentally?" I quip, my palms starting to sweat.

"The bannister's pretty wide, it'll drop you right down on the hill. Then all you have to focus on is keeping your balance—or falling really well."

I approach the edge, my numb feet barely registering the slick concrete.

"So..." I balance the tray on the bannister.

"I know you can do this, Nan."

I can picture all of the broken bones waiting for me on this hill, all the potential concussions and minor deaths. But I've been through worse than this. I had a fucking machine in my brain, I've been manipulated and sidelined and used. A broken bone is better than any of those things.

And I can feel a readiness in me, a thirst to do this because I want to. Not for Marius. Not for Yarro, not for Jessica or Reena or Adam.

For me.

The top of the tray sticks out over the edge of the concrete. It gleams in the weak moonlight that reaches the clear strip of land. The snow glows all the way down.

Treating the tray like a snowboard, I turn my back foot, steadying myself. A deep breath, sharp air cutting all the way down my windpipe. I ready my other foot on the cafeteria tray, slide it forward—

The world tips and rushes at me, the tray grating down the icy bannister—*oh shit oh shit oh shit oh shit oh SHIT!*—I shift my weight down into my knees as the tray skims over snow, flinging my arms out to grasp at anything, anything!

Yarro is shouting—the snowy hill comes up at me, the trees bend back. The tray slides ahead and I slide with it, and Christ, the wind feels incredible. My ears burn cold, and a sound bubbles up out of me, a laugh or a sob, maybe both.

All too soon, the world catches up and grabs hold. Slows me down until I am standing in one place. The tray settles underneath me in the snow.

"That was fucking amazing!" Yarro shouts down the hill.

Every part of my body is tingling with adrenaline. The shadows on the snow are solid enough to believe in.

I pick up the tray and make my way back up the hill.

CHAPTER THIRTY-TWO
Tattoos

"YOUR CLOTHES'LL BE dry in about an hour."

"Thanks."

Yarro opens a cupboard above the stove. "Hot chocolate? I have coffee, and tea, somewhere." They pull down a red canister, a couple of cartons.

"Hot chocolate sounds good."

Yarro flicks the tab on a silver kettle and opens another cupboard.

Their apartment is a one-bedroom deal, the kitchen separated from the living room by a framed counter.

Thawing on the long section of their L-shaped couch, I watch as Yarro goes through the ritual of making instant hot chocolate. They've changed into a black t-shirt and plaid pajama pants, similar to the outfit they've lent me while my clothes dry.

My thawing toes curl in the thick, green carpet. A rack of potted plants sits in front of the double-paned windows overlooking downtown. Paperbacks and knickknacks fill the shelf that runs the entire circumference of the living room. A striped armchair sits comfortably in the corner. It's almost familiar.

Yarro sets two mugs on the coffee table, a padded bench with the top flipped over to reveal a wood inset. They settle on the short part of the L-couch, resting their arm along the cushioned back.

Claiming one of the mugs, I blow across the top. "Did it come that way?" I ask about their tattooed hand.

Yarro smiles at me. "No, I ordered it plain. When it came in, I dropped it off at a tattoo place, and they got it back to me in a couple of weeks. Pretty quick, considering the work I asked for."

"Didn't it hurt when you attached it?"

"Oh, like hell." They lean forward to pick up their mug. "What about yours? Something happen to the original?"

I test the hot chocolate—it's perfectly warm and sweet as the liquid coats my tongue.

"I don't really know. The original got switched at some point. I found out, got rid of its replacement. This one's secondhand."

Yarro places their hot chocolate back on the table. "I don't want to ask questions if it makes you uncomfortable."

"I don't know how many I can answer right now." I take another comforting sip. "Maybe later?"

Nodding, Yarro stares at a distant spot on the carpet. Then they look up with the same lopsided smile from the bar.

"Wanna trade?"

I remove my secondhand hand, and place it on Yarro's knee. Even if everything up 'til now was a trick, I can trust my own body—I've never been able to disjoin my hand that easily before.

Yarro disconnects their tattooed hand and holds it in front of me. I lift my arm to it, feel the joint *shhhk* into place. The hand's comically large on my too-thin wrist. I turn it over, palm up. I realise the tattoos encircling each of the fingers are strings of words.

"Old poems," Yarro says, shifting closer to me. Their finger traces the words with my secondhand hand, I feel their touch over the tattooed skin. "'Your love is more delightful than wine'…. 'your name is like perfume poured out'…. 'My beloved is to me a cluster of henna blossoms from the vineyards of En Gedi.' Shit like that. I can read them and think those things are about me too. '*My* breasts are towers,' strong, resilient. '*My* name is like perfume.' Someone is saying these things to me. But this one's a reminder," they gently turn the hand over, my breath catching at the warmth radiating from their palms. "'Do not arouse or awaken love until it so desires.'"

Yarro's eyes search mine. "I know you don't remember. I don't want you to feel pressured in any way. That's why I called Sid an asshole for making jokes, but that wasn't really fair, he didn't know. I guess when I saw you at the bar…I just wanted to do one more crazy thing with you. And that was unfair of me, because maybe you wanted to forget me, and that's why you changed your face."

Without thinking, my left hand reaches across to settle on their cheek. "I get to choose which parts I bring into the future."

My lips find Yarro's. My body shifts up against theirs. They wrap their arms around my shoulders.

We find new, familiar places as Yarro slowly rubs our hands over my back, as if waking me up from a dream.

CHAPTER THIRTY-THREE
Ends of My Hair

WE'RE BOTH STARVING, so we head out, the lining in our jackets holding warmth from the dryer. Yarro takes off their wool gloves as we reach the 24-hour sandwich shop. An electric bell rings somewhere in the back. Even though it's late, the tables are all full of people with hands cupped around styrofoam coffee cups, couples sharing subs, a study group with open books and laptops between crumpled napkins and pop cans.

Yarro goes up to the cashier, who has a bright yellow apron tied over their collared shirt. Their black hair is slicked back under a hairnet.

"Hey Alex, how's your shift going?"

"Please, don't ask," they roll their eyes.

"Then I'll have a B.L.T on rye." Yarro turns to me, but I shake my head, fishing for my wallet. "And a gingersnap cookie, please."

"Cool," Alex takes the 20 from Yarro and picks change out of the cash drawer. "And for you?"

I step up to the counter, at a loss. "Ham and cheese?"

"What kind of bread?"

"Whole wheat, if you have it."

"Seven-ninety-five."

I pay with the debit card in my wallet. I wonder how much money is on it, how much of it is from *Shady Hut*. As I watch Alex layer vegetables and cold cuts, I resolve to quit, feeling lighter as I return the wallet in my coat pocket.

We eat at the tall table facing the front window. An occasional car drives through the slushy street. Yarro reaches for my hand, holding onto it as we chew through our sandwiches.

"So," I say between bites. "Tell me something about you that I don't know."

Yarro squeezes my hand. "That could be anything."

"Correct." I start on the second half of my sandwich.

"Where I work?"

"No idea."

"The Rehabilitation Centre for Damaged Parts?"

"Tell me about it."

Yarro lets go of my hand and piles their empty sandwich paper and napkins onto the small plastic tray. "It's literal pain—eight hours a day, four days a week. I've been working on a broken leg for the past month. The femur was splintered when I got it. Lots of relaxed weight bearing, short walks, that kind of thing." Yarro picks up their gingersnap cookie. "Anybody can work there, and the pay isn't bad. Free meals while we're there too, and vitamins. Real parts are still necessary to the industry, and this way nothing gets wasted. Some parts go back into the hospital system. Corporations buy some for retail. That's not great, to be honest, but I'd rather the parts get reused than thrown out. Besides, you meet interesting people. Not many stay very long, though. The pain wears them out."

For a moment, Yarro's face turns grim. They take a bite of the gingersnap, the act of chewing bringing them out of it. "My favourite part is just leaving work at work, y'know? When I worked at the restaurant, my boss would send emails out at midnight listing all of the things the day staff did wrong, right down to setting out the wrong kind of fork. I mean, it was a minimum wage job, not worth the stress."

I fold up my empty sandwich paper. "Ever get something really broken? Like, bullet holes or something?"

Yarro brushes their hands on their cargo pants. "I had a perforated lung one time. Was too far gone. You can't save everything."

The weight of the statement settles over us. Snow starts falling in the street. A van drives by.

"I found a Polaroid. Of you." My cheeks get warm. "That's why I noticed you at the bar."

Yarro frowns, embarrassed. "Shit."

"What?"

"When you stopped answering my texts…You weren't staying at your usual spots, so I went to your mom's place." They sigh and lace their fingers together, the tattoos intertwining. "She wouldn't let me in— something was sus about that, right? I was worried. You'd sent me the garage door code that one time your mom was out of town, so…I came back the next day and went up to your room. All your stuff was gone. I thought maybe you'd moved, got that new start you wanted. But you left the nightstand key under the lamp, like you always did. And I had the photo in my bag. You took it last summer. I thought maybe if you came home to visit, you'd find it and, I dunno, call me or something. It was really stupid."

My throat gets tight. Yarro's face goes blurry as I blink tears from my eyes. "You tried to find me."

Yarro rubs my shoulder. "Of course I did."

"You thought I left without telling you…"

"Doesn't matter now." Their bright expression flushes my cheeks. "You're back, and we can work on getting your memory back, too, amnesia be damned." Yarro rubs my shoulder one more time and hops off their stool. "I'm getting a coffee, want anything?"

"I'm good."

As Yarro heads to the counter, I turn back to the window, resting my chin in my second-hand hand. A warmth permeates my body, spreading through every limb, the ends of my hair. I can't remember the last time I felt this comfortable. This safe. My gaze drifts over the half-lit apartment blocks and the row of abandoned storefronts.

A figure crosses the street at a jagged angle, blunt haircut blowing over her face.

I recognise her. Not from before. From recently. The stature, the caramel coat, the silhouette of her hair—I'm positive it's the sales clerk from *High Five*.

"Nan?" Yarro's voice stops me at the door.

"Sorry," I apologise, getting ready to turn around and run after Amber.

"What the hell!"

"Just something I gotta check out. I'll be back, I promise."

"You bastard," they laugh, hurt.

"Promise!" I wrench the door open.

The cold shocks me into motion. I pump my legs and round the corner, just in time to see Amber duck past an old shawarma shop. I trail her down a side street. After a few blocks she turns into another alley.

Halfway down the gloomy corridor, I realise that it leads to *High Five*. Before I can reach her, Amber unlocks the boutique's alley door and goes inside.

CHAPTER THIRTY-FOUR
Disembodied

I DUCK BEHIND a pile of discarded crates and catch my breath. Back against the brick wall, I monitor the metal side door through the latticed plastic. It feels weird to be staking out a person I don't even know, but my guess is that it's around 3 a.m. No way a sales clerk is doing overtime this late on a Saturday.

And there's something else, too. A buzzing in my skull that started when I saw Amber cross the street, something telling me that this is *it*—what it's all leading to.

I wait, Yarro's injured expression fresh in my memory.

High Five's side door is cold steel, a hooded bulb flickering over it like a drunken eye about to pass out, casting an uneasy pool of light over the ice-sheen concrete. An open pipe runs up the wall across from it, plugs spilling out of the plastic rim like tentacles. A stack of flattened cardboard boxes shudders as something passes underneath. Half-frozen water fills a low point in the concrete, shimmering as snowflakes fall into it, saturate, and sink. Just beyond, I can make out something that reminds me of a disembodied shin. You'd have to be pretty desperate to pick up a part like that, discarded in an alley in the middle of the night, nibbled at by strays.

The wind dies down. The alley goes crystal still. If someone leaves out the front door, I'll be able to hear the overhead bell.

Jessica's place is mere blocks away, but if I go now, I might miss Amber leaving.

Thick snowflakes start to fall around me, hitting my coat sleeve and sticking before melting away. Others drift into the grungy brick wall like cotton poplar seeds. I imagine spring. The whir of lawnmowers, the calls of red-winged blackbirds passing through my childhood backyard. The tricky smell of bread emanating from the brewery district. A time before this harrowing winter.

Snowflakes bounce down the brick wall and shimmer to the gutter. *Christ, what is it all for?*

Sharp cold against my cheeks, sweat under my jacket, numbness seeping into my ears. Each exhale covers my eyes in condensation, a veil that clears to reveal the same littered alley. Snowflakes build a small line of silver where brick meets concrete.

The scuff of feet on pavement—someone turns into the alley. The steps are measured, unhurried. I'm far enough away that the hooded light over the side door doesn't reach me. I can only hope the stack of crates is enough cover.

The figure slows, stepping into the lit circle. My breath catches: it's Reena. No coat, just a red hoodie, black sweatpants, slip-on winter boots. She bangs twice on the metal door with her fist and steps back. She waits, like a stone at the bottom of a pool.

Amber opens the door. Another figure exits behind her, wearing dress pants and a fitted ski jacket cut to their waist. His shoes gleam like obsidian in the snow.

A face materialises out of the shadows: a youthful face, but not young. There's something unsettling about the rosy skin, the raw hazel eyes. Even from this distance, I can tell that his face is completely symmetrical, something only attained by constant body manipulation and access to high-quality parts.

The man with the symmetrical face takes a step towards Reena, who has shrunk away to the edge of the light.

"We've been looking for you for a long time, Maria." The man's commanding voice resonates through the alley.

"You're him, aren't you? The Father." Reena straightens, the shadows cast away. "You've changed yourself. Isn't that against the Essentialist code?"

"'We are born our true selves,'" he intones. "But I don't think there's any harm in maintaining one's youth, do you?"

"Hypocrite." Reena spits the word. "What do you want?"

"I'd think that'd be obvious, after I put so much effort into this reverse scavenger hunt. You didn't have to look for the fingers. They found you."

"They're from a child." Reena's expression brims over with contempt. "Even you must know that what you're doing is wrong."

The symmetrical man is unphased. "A very special child." He takes a thumb from the lapel of his coat. "Did you ever wonder why you were kept in that room, away from the other Mothers? You were special. You still are." He holds out the thumb, his eyes on

Reena's face. "Do you know what this is? A miracle. A little girl in a room all alone, regenerating her fingers."

Reena winces, her hands gripping into fists. "They're...mine?"

"Yes. I was worried that you had forgotten all about us, but I did what I could to jog your memory. It will be so nice to have the family back together again, Maria."

"That isn't my name." Reena's voice is low, her gaze focusing past the man, past the alley.

The symmetrical man becomes engrossed with the thumb in his grasp. "These fingers... I have dozens more of them. We'd remove one from your hand, and another would grow in to replace it before the day was out. You were a very good child. You never let your mouth grow back in, you knew it would be wrong to go against my wishes. But then you pulled that *stunt*—" His round, white teeth clench together. "But that's all over now. We can bring you back into the fold. You can unlock humanity's potential, with your gift."

Reena shakes her head slowly. "I'm not like that anymore." Her gaze snaps back to the symmetrical man. "Even if you go through the trouble of dragging me back, I will be of no use to you. Leave me in peace."

"I believe that your regenerative tendencies have improved with age." The man ignores her and returns the thumb to his lapel pocket. "These kid parts, they were enough to unlock the door to synthetic production. But with adult regeneration—there would be no limits."

"Why aren't you in prison?" Reena demands.

The symmetrical man sighs, as if dealing with a stubborn child. "One of our delivery people reported us. So ungrateful. Only a few managed to get away. But we have powerful friends. Like Marius. Oh, you know Marius, don't you? An excellent business man. Discreet."

"But I saw it on the news. They freed all the Mothers."

"Come with me, Maria."

"Don't call me that!" Reena growls, her face resolute.

"After all the work I put into finding you?" The disappointment in the man's perfect face feels staged. "I'm hurt."

"I'm not like that anymore," Reena repeats steadily.

"I wish I could just take you at your word, but you must understand—I need *absolute* proof."

Amber moves to stand by the man, her hand reaching into her bag.

"Do you know that with your regenerative tissue, we could monopolise the parts market? We could change how people buy, how they consume."

The symmetrical man's eyes positively shine with greed.

"The body is a wonderful commodity. People will always need it, always want to upgrade, stay young, look beautiful. And you're going to help me, whether you like it or not. Amber?" He turns to the sales clerk. "*In the side.*"

The phrase hits me like a lightning strike. My body launches to its feet, an absent hand grasping for—

They're going to see you! my instincts scream. I duck behind the crates. What the hell was that?

A firework goes off. No—

The gun in Amber's hand.

Reena grunts and buckles onto the icy concrete.

Amber pockets the gun as the symmetrical man walks over to Reena's crumpled form. He leans over her, his face full of calm anticipation. "Heal yourself," he says.

Reena groans. Blood splatters her sweater and the thin snow in the alley. She rolls onto her back, the solid mountain of her body struggling to breathe. Fluttering hands try to find the leak.

The hooded light bulb flickers. The symmetrical man's hazel eyes flash from shadowed eye sockets. After a long moment, he straightens up, accepting. "There was always this possibility," his voice is clinical. "You'll live out your last minutes bleeding to death in this alley, as you deserve. We'll just have to make do with the parts we have."

Obsidian shoes step around Reena's body as the symmetrical man moves out of the light. The final slam of a car door echoes from the street. The squeal of getaway tires as the symmetrical man disappears into the urban maze. The city swallows him whole.

The sales clerk, Amber, stays behind. As the sound of the car engine merges into the city, she shakes her head and blinks a few times. Her gaze freezes on Reena's prone body, the growing circle of red on the ground.

"Oh my god, are you okay?" Amber yells. She absently smooths the back of her hair. "I...I can call..." She takes her cell phone out of her pocket, but seems unable to do anything with it. "Oh...something isn't...Fuck!"

Reena's groans fill the alley.

Amber turns back to the side door, searching for her keys. Nothing comes up. Tears fill her three eyes as she stamps the ground in frustration. Suddenly, Amber bolts through the darkness and is gone.

CHAPTER THIRTY-FIVE
Goes to Pieces

UP UNTIL THIS moment, I've never thought of Reena as someone who could be held. The idea of Jessica giving her a hug, or Adam rubbing her back like he rubbed mine after the secondhand store—there's something almost obscene about it.

Yet, here I am, kneeling next to her, my hand gripping one of hers. Holding onto her for dear life. Blood has dyed the bottom half of her hoodie a black-red.

"You can let go," says a voice. It takes me a second to register the sound: the soft words are Reena's.

I lower her arm so that it's resting across my jeans instead of draping down into the snow. Why is the snow so red?

Her blue gaze finds mine, a kind of relief relaxing her brow.

There are no phones, I panic. My cell phone is gone, abandoned on that park bench days ago. I can't leave her. She needs an ambulance. "I don't know what to do," I confide, tears stinging my eyes.

And for the first time, Reena smiles at me. A real, warm smile that offers understanding, but no answers.

I become aware that my right hand is pressing my rolled up scarf against the bullet wound in her side. I don't remember deciding to do that, but somehow, it was done.

"Help!" I call, but the alleyway is empty. "Help! She's been shot!"

Reena's eyelids slip closed. Her jaw shifts.

Someone runs through the alley, upsetting boxes and garbage cans. Old shingles and metal scrap clatter in their wake.

Adam reaches us, knees showing through his frayed cargo pants. He collapses on the other side of Reena, his breath coming in stuttering gasps. He takes in the blood flowing out from under my hand, the way Reena's serious smile turns to him with sickening finality.

He flips open his ancient cell phone, types in three numbers, holds it to his ear, his free hand smoothing Reena's short hair. His voice sounds far away as it describes Reena's injury, our location.

The phone snaps shut and he drops it, his other hand pressing on top of mine, on top of the blood. "I found the note on the table—you shouldn't have come alone!"

"The death of the body is nothing to fear," Reena whispers.

Adam weeps silently, the lump in his throat lifting. But he can't hide his eyes, the trembling around his mouth. "Of course it is!" he bursts out with a kind of laugh, taking Reena's shoulders.

Her eyelids slip closed, and then her cold, beautiful eyes flash open as if in argument—

She loses control of her bladder. She loses control of everything. There is no control. Her body parts come off in his hands. Her face is chaos. Nothing holds the pieces together anymore.

I turn from it, covering my face with my hands. The darkness reeks of blood.

When I emerge, Adam is still gripping Reena's shoulders even though they're dislocated inside the sleeves of her red hoodie.

The alley closes in around us: the sudden absence and the still-warm body, the uncanny sense that her mouth could close at any moment—knowing it never will.

CHAPTER THIRTY-SIX
Gone

I PICK ADAM'S phone off the ground. Select Jessica's number.

It rings twice before she answers. "Adam?"

"It's me," I say. "It's Nan."

"Is everything alright? I hear sirens."

"Reena's hurt." The words hang in the air. I'm unable to change my answer to something more truthful.

"Where are you?"

"The alley, the alley we waited in."

When I don't elaborate, she says, "I'm on my way."

As the police section off the alley, Jessica's rapid footsteps round the corner. Her breath goes up like smoke in front of her.

"I know who did this!" she shouts at a passing police officer. "It was Marius! Investigate him, for the love of God!" She spots me and rushes over. "Where's Reena, did they take her to the hospital? How hurt is she?" Her features are sharp and angry, her mouth pressed in a line.

My bloodied fingers grasp at the beige shoulder of her trench coat.

She spots Adam past the police tape. Jessica frees herself from my grip, ducks under the tape, and stares down the officer who approaches her. The buzzing in my ears cancels out their conversation.

Finally, Jessica turns around and sees what's left of Reena.

CHAPTER THIRTY-SEVEN
Redistributed

THEY HOLD REENA'S funeral at a meditation centre. The inside of the low building is all hardwood and windows, like a long banquet hall. Rows of metal fold-out chairs face one end of the room. A red backdrop curtain runs the length of the wall underneath a round window circling a piece of blue sky.

I can't remember if I've been to many funerals, but this one feels about the same as any of the others. People stand in knotted clusters, hands patting backs, subdued voices, some tears. A thin display stand at the front of the room supports a clear dome. Encased inside is a black felt bag.

Jessica and Adam are in one of the clusters. Adam hunches over to hear what the person next to him is saying. Jessica's mouth is set in a grimace.

A chime rings, respectfully—a two minute warning. Clusters break apart and morph into lines, threading into the rows of seating. I claim a chair near the end of the second row. Jessica and Adam wordlessly sit on either side of me.

Jessica takes my hand as a bald person in a simple white dress approaches the clear dome.

"Reena has moved on from here," their voice rings off the hardwood up to the ceiling. "She has no further need for her body. Parts of it will continue on in this world, and will be redistributed to those with the most need, as is tradition. Her brain will be cremated to show our appreciation for her contribution to our community, and to recognize her individual experiences as hers alone, never to be shared by another. There is one other piece, however, that will remain hers alone." The speaker refers to the dome, the black felt bag. "On her donor card, Reena expressed her wish that her mouth be cremated as well. We honour that wish today." They look out at the crowd of people and nod to someone in the front row. Standing quietly, Jessica and Adam move to join the person and the speaker by the dome.

"We also honour Reena's family: Lin, Jessica, and Adam." The speaker turns to face the three of them. "I have known Reena since she moved to this city as a teenager," the speaker continues. "She had a fierce and loving spirit, and carried herself with dignity and compassion. She worked hard to ease the suffering of others and brought joy to all of us. She will greatly be missed here."

Turning, the speaker addresses the room for the last time. "I'm sure her family would appreciate hearing your stories about Reena, and how she touched your lives. There will be a reception following in the adjoining room for that purpose." The speaker grips Jessica's hand before taking a seat.

Absolute silence fills the hall. Jessica and Adam support each other, eyes on the black felt bag under the clear dome. Stepping forward, Lin places a hand on the back of the display stand and presses a button. The dome flashes white and fills with curling smoke that masks the bag and the pale flame engulfing it. A song comes on over the loudspeaker, a chorus of wood flutes and harps, a deep ancient melody. After a few moments, the smoke clears, ventilated down through the display stand. The inside of the dome is empty.

Dozens of chair legs stutter across the floor as most of the room stands. I stand with them, silent and still, until the song comes to an end.

CHAPTER THIRTY-EIGHT
Holding it Together

JESSICA, ADAM, AND I sit around the fold-out table, each of us staring at some point on the wall. Hard to remember what day it is—did I meet Yarro last night or weeks ago? Did Reena just die, or has she been dead for a year?

A migraine pushes on the inside of my skull; my eyes are sore, dried out. Across the table, Adam is a mirror image of how I feel, his eyes open too wide, a tendon flexing in his jaw.

Jessica's gaze hasn't left the art wall in hours. Her features are soft, as if the past few days have taken a sander to her usually sharp expression. Both of her hands lay disconnected on the table—an old tradition, removing hands or feet, a cathartic way to sit with loss.

Grief-weary, I get up using the table as support, and make my way to the kitchen to turn on the coffee maker. Small things like this take crazy amounts of energy. Pushing through the thick silence with a word is a near-impossible task that all three of us have decidedly given up.

I pinch the coffee scoop handle, scrape the bottom of the canister. There's dirt under my fingernails, or maybe it's grounds from the three days of sitting, where all we can do is drink coffee. There's a cut healing over my third knuckle. Don't remember how I got it. Should bandage it.

I pour the last of the grounds directly into the plastic filter and swing it closed. A red light clicks on, the element inside whirring as it heats the water and pushes it up through the machine. A single stream of coffee hits the bottom of the glass pot, splattering up the sides, the volume increasing to the 1 cup line, then 2 cups, then 3. The coffeemaker sputters into silence. The red light clicks off.

I pour two cups, take them to Jessica and Adam, then pour one for myself.

Adam reaches for the sugar bowl in the middle of the table. He removes the lid and uses the spoon inside to ferry three scoops of sugar to his mug.

The click of metal as he stirs draws Jessica out of her staring. Clearing her throat, she says "The police station called. A new investigator wants to talk with us."

I sit down next to her. "We already gave our statements about what happened."

Adam runs a hand over his face. His hoodie hangs from his bowed shoulders like a dead sail. "Marius has police protection. What good's another statement going to do?"

Jessica slumps deeper into the chair, the corners of her mouth drooping.

A sudden knock on the door shakes our guts, startles us half out of our seats.

Jessica's shoulders arch, on alert. She waits for a moment, then quickly extends her arms to reconnect with her disembodied hands. She grips them into fists a couple of times, then takes her coffee mug with her as she rounds the corner into the entryway.

Adam uses her wake to propel him into the back hallway. His bedroom door creaks on its hinges as it swings shut.

I sit with my mug, waiting. I listen as Jessica unlocks the deadbolt, turns the handle.

"Oh Erna!" Jessica exclaims, her voice almost tender. "Come in, yes of course, I'm afraid I forgot…"

Jessica comes around the corner and pulls out a chair from the end of the table.

A wide, grey-haired person totters into view, a set of wire-framed glasses pushed right up to his slightly bulging eyes.

"Wanna coffee?" Jessica asks as he settles into the chair.

"No, no, I'm just on my way through. Hello," he says to me. "I'm Erna."

"Nan."

"Nan!" Erna says, folding his hands on the table, "That's a name you don't hear much anymore. Very nice to meet you."

"It's all ready for you, Erna." Jessica leaves her coffee mug on the table, moving into the hallway.

"Is Reena here?" Erna looks out the patio door.

Jessica stops in front of Reena's bedroom, her black sweater and jeans seeming to weigh her in place. "She's out today," Jessica lies, "but I'll be sure to tell her hello."

Erna sighs, disappointed. "I wanted to thank her personally for all her work. It wasn't an easy thing I asked her to do."

"I'll get it for you." Jessica pauses a moment before pushing Reena's bedroom door open.

Erna taps his fingers on the back of his other hand, keeping time to a song I can't hear. "They say a thaw's coming," he says suddenly. "Going to be plus ten."

"That's good." I sip at the coffee. It's bitter, but I don't care.

"Always nice to see the spring starting. The leaves come out, the birds return from wherever they've been. It's like a reunion. Have you ever woken up in a tent?"

"Like, camping?" I ask, uncertain of what else to say.

He nods, staring out the window. "It's cold in the mornings, and you just want to stay bundled in your sleeping bag. The birds start singing at 5 a.m., and you're so mad at them because it's too damn early for that kind of thing. But then it gets quiet and the sun rises fully, and there's all this light coming through the tent, and you get up, but only because you have to pee, and you unzip the front of the tent—" He closes his eyes, and the decades tumble from his face, gather in his upturned hands. "Outside is so still, and green, with trees all around, ancient trees. And the air is fresh and the coals from last night's fire are still warm. That's what spring feels like."

Reena's door closes, and Jessica comes out of the hall, carrying a garment bag high in front of her.

"Oooh, how exciting!" Erna exclaims, pushing himself slowly from the chair. "Can I see it?"

Jessica holds the garment bag up for Erna to unzip. Inside is the wedding dress from Reena's room.

"It's beautiful." His bottom lip starts to quiver, his grey-green eyes shining. "Just like the day we were married."

"I'm sure it will be a wonderful anniversary surprise."

"Things were so different back then." Erna takes a folded up tissue from his pocket. "Zane and I showed up at City Hall in matching dresses, and they wouldn't let us in. Zane said we would wait outside the building for as long as it took, until they would marry us." Erna laughs a little at the memory. "And we did wait, all night, on the steps in our wedding dresses. Someone from the TV station came to interview us, but by then City Hall gave in, and we were married." He dabs his eyes, lowers the tissue. "Zane will be so surprised when I show up to our party in the same dress from 50 years ago." Erna takes an envelope from the pocket of his winter jacket. "Please tell Reena it means the world to me."

Jessica holds up her free hand. "I can't accept that, Erna."

But he insists, placing it on the table. "Make sure Reena gets this," he tells me, thinking Jessica is only being polite.

I look to Jessica, who's barely holding it together. "I will."

"Well, I should be going. Lots to get ready for tonight. It was very nice to meet you, Nan."

Jessica zips up the garment bag. "Let me carry this down to your car."

"Thank you. I just replaced my knees six months ago and they're already catching up to the rest of me."

Jessica pulls on her boots and the two of them leave. Faint footsteps descend the fire escape.

Adam's bedroom door opens. He matches my eyes, but doesn't say anything. Retreating back inside, he closes the door.

Silence settles around me. I take a deep breath all the way down to my diaphragm. An envelope with Reena's name sits at my elbow.

What is it all for?

I sip at the coffee.

Heavy footsteps clang up the fire escape. The front door creaks and slams. Jessica stomps past the art wall, across the apartment, into her bedroom. She pulls the door shut behind her. A few muffled sobs carry down the hall.

I finish my coffee. Clear the half-full mugs from the table. Pour the cold liquid down the sink. I wash the mugs and set them in the draining tray.

A scratching starts up in the entryway. It takes a few minutes to register the noise as something I can investigate.

Thank Christ—something besides the endless questions. Something that I can find an answer to.

I follow the scraping to its source and open the apartment door. No Name takes his time coming in, as if it wasn't what he wanted all along.

CHAPTER THIRTY-NINE
On the Other Hand

ON THE THIRD floor of the police department, we occupy the only bank of chairs lining the long hallway. Adam reads a yellow hardcover book. Jessica has one of her hands clenched in a fist on her knee. The door across from us is labelled "Special Operations." The gold plaque glints in such a way I can't read the name underneath.

I pretend to check the time on my new phone, really checking to see if Yarro replied to my text. There are four numbers in my contacts now: 'Jessica', 'Adam', 'Mom', and 'Yarro'.

I found Yarro's number a couple of days ago, tucked into the pocket of my jacket. They must've slipped it in when they took it out of the dryer. I feel like it's a good sign, but that was before I ditched them at the sandwich shop.

So much has happened since then.

Thinking about Yarro digs a hollow in my chest. I check my phone again. No new messages.

A tall administrator in a blue suit stops at the "Special Operations" door and knocks. Jessica, Adam, and I lean forward. After a moment, they go into the office and shut us out. Hushed voices sift under the door.

A few minutes pass before they reemerge from the office. "She's ready for you." They continue down the hallway to a stairwell, their heels clicking along the tiled floor.

Jessica rises, her stride steady, her eyes alert. Adam follows with difficulty, like a ship trying to tack against the wind.

I go last and wait in the doorway. Jessica and Adam sit in chairs facing a massive desk covered in neat stacks of papers and files, all labelled with bright blue, pink, and yellow sticky notes. The person on the other side of the desk occupies a high-backed wooden chair, but she makes it look like the most comfortable place to be in the world. He has an ease about him, the ability to lounge without losing their impeccable posture.

"I'm Special Agent Deborah Alard, please feel free to use any pronouns." His hair is almost black, long and teased, with voluminous bangs arching over their walnut-brown forehead. Her brown eyes gleam with interest. "Please close the door, Nan."

Startled, I pull the door shut and hurry to join Jessica and Adam.

"You read our statements," Jessica says for my benefit.

"Exactly." Agent Alard leans forward, and gives us each a look. "It's good to put people to the names. I've been over your file many times." They pause for a moment, noticing Adam's worn expression. "I'm sorry for your loss."

"Thank you," Jessica says, shifting herself forward in the chair. "I don't mean to be rude, but it's been a very difficult week for us."

"Of course." Agent Alard places a hand on top of the largest stack of files. "I want you to know that I've been specially assigned to this case, and many others like it. I fully intend to investigate everything you've mentioned in your statements. And everything you've tried to bring to our attention in the past."

Jessica's eyes flash. "The police discarded the case about that kid, they said there wasn't enough evidence."

"They lied."

"But—"

"The Chief of Police has resigned and half of the local force is under investigation. The turnover was bound to happen once Head Office had evidence of corruption. Bribery, forgery, blackmail. It's sordid stuff. I was assigned to come in and take over reports of stolen or forcefully removed body parts, blackmarket distribution lines, and brain tampering." Agent Alard's eyes flash in my direction, her eyelids lifting slightly. "Your case seems to fit all of these requirements."

He takes a small microphone from a drawer and sets it on a pile of papers in the middle of the desk. "I know this is a difficult thing to ask, since you've already had to talk to so many people and give so many statements, so I ask you, sincerely: will you tell me what happened? There's no way for me to know what was left off the record, and the possibility for tampering is definitely one I cannot rule out. If you're willing to tell me everything, it could help immensely with the investigation."

"You said there are other cases like this one?" I say, bile rising in my throat. "Marius did this to other people?"

Agent Alard nods seriously. "His name was left off all of the official records as a potential suspect. There's a high chance that he's been doing this for a long time and bribing the police not to implicate him. He and one of his employees," they check a sticky note, "Amber, appear to have skipped town. Seems pretty suspicious to me."

"Yes." I wait for Jessica and Adam's reactions.

Adam slouches in his chair, but Jessica's eyes are raging. "We'll tell you everything we can."

Agent Alard claps their hands once, xyr smile widening into a determined grin. "Excellent, thank you. I'd like to start with Adam, if you don't mind, and then I'll interview Jessica, and Nan last. You're both welcome to wait outside, or there's a little cafeteria on the main floor. I promise no one will bother you. I'll send Adam out once we've had our chat."

Agent Alard walks Jessica and I to the doorway; Adam waits in his seat with vacant eyes.

"See you soon." Agent Alard closes the door.

An hour passes waiting outside the office. We try not to listen to the hum of Adam's voice under the door, the long silences between.

Starting to feel hungry, Jessica and I make our way downstairs and find the cafeteria. There's a little window to request items from the chalkboard menu, and a cluster of tables and plastic chairs to eat at.

The cashier is a cheerful person with freckles all over their arms. "Here's your order!" they say, setting a tray of coffee and boxed sandwiches between us.

"Thanks," Jessica mumbles.

The cashier takes our order number placard and moves away.

Springing open the plastic carton, Jessica picks up the triangle of bread with lettuce, turkey, and cheese layered inside. She takes a bite. Overcome with hunger, she scarfs the rest down, like a hawk eating a mouse.

I stifle a laugh, and she looks up, slowing down to chew the last half of the sandwich.

"That was the best thing I've ever eaten," she says, pushing the plastic box to the side and focusing on her coffee.

I take my first bite—the bread is stale, the lettuce limp. "You haven't been eating." I swallow painfully.

Her mouth curls at the corners, nearly smiling at my culinary pain.

"Do you think we can trust Agent Alard?"

Jessica's shoulders square as she sees Adam come down the staircase. "They're the best chance we have."

She takes her coffee with her, meeting Adam halfway. She grips his arm, and he nods, finding me from across the room. Jessica heads up the stairs.

Adam settles into the seat across from me. He rests the yellow hardcover book facedown on the table, bags under his eyes like raised plaster.

"Hey." I push the other half of my sandwich over to him.

"Hey." After a moment he picks up the flat triangle and takes a bite. "This is good."

"No, it's not."

"No. It's not." His face lifts, a kind of irony diffusing through it, the closest thing to a smile he can manage.

"How was it?" I ask about upstairs.

He takes another bite of the sandwich, and swallows, his adam's apple rising and falling as he forces the food down. "I think Alard knows what she's doing."

"Yeah?"

"Yeah." He puts the rest of the sandwich on the tray, brushing the crumbs from his sweater. "Xe asked about the note."

Adam's voice echoes through my memory: *I found the note on the table...* "I thought you didn't tell anyone—"

"I didn't. Alard wanted to know why Reena went to the *High Five* that night. Said it was really important. I told him that I was out and when I got home—someone must've delivered it, then Reena left the note behind—" He covers his face briefly, takes a deep breath. "If only I'd been there sooner."

"She didn't want anyone else to get hurt," I say through the catch in my throat. "It's not your fault."

"Not yours either." His words carry extra weight, and we both shut up for a while, staring at the empty sandwich shells.

"I wanted to tell you," Adam says. "I'm going to be heading out soon."

"Well, your interview's done. I'll see you at the apartment."

His fingers pick at a piece of tape holding the book's spine together. "I mean, I'll be leaving. It's almost spring, and there's a place I have to go." He closes his eyes. "I won't be back for a while."

"Oh." I realise how much I'm going to miss him. "Right."

"But I'm glad Mom won't be alone," he opens his eyes and actually smiles, the warmth of it filling his features. "And neither will you, Nan-for-now."

"Nan for keeps," I say, feeling good and right saying it.

Adam reaches over for my hand. I grip his in return. It's nothing like I thought this moment would be—holding hands with Adam. Whatever I wanted us to be before, we're something else now. And Christ, I hold onto that, as tightly as I can.

The moment passes. Adam picks up the yellow hardcover and flips to a bookmarked page.

I open the message I sent to Yarro and read it over for the one thousandth time:

Hey, it's Nan. I'm sorry about the other night.

Should I elaborate? Try to explain why I had to go, that it was a weird brain programming thing? That I knew Amber was up to something, that she was carrying out what Marius had originally planned for me? That's why I jumped up when the symmetrical man said "In the side": I was supposed to be the one pulling the trigger. I haven't talked to Adam or Jessica about it, but we all know the truth. I'm just glad that Mr. Snaff got the machine out of me in time. But I can't tell Yarro all of that, it'll sound crazy, they'll think I'm making excuses—

My phone buzzes in my hand and a message icon pops up. It's from Yarro. Without opening it, I read the text preview:

I didn't think that...

...what? "I didn't think you'd be such an asshole?" "I didn't think that you'd leave again?" That twists me up; I almost give into the nausea. Instead, I open the message:

I didn't think that you'd text me. You seemed pretty eager to leave.

I type and delete a dozen different answers, trying to think of how to explain. I finally settle on the truest response I can think of.

I miss you.

Is that enough? I think about it for another minute, then add:

I know more about what happened to me now. The amnesia stuff. It's a lot to explain. But I shouldn't have run out on you like that.

I close the phone and stuff it in my pocket before I type something else stupid.

Adam sets down his book, glancing over my shoulder. "You're up," he says.

Jessica reaches the table and takes one of the free chairs. She looks worn out, a hawk landing after a long flight.

"I'll be here when you're done," she says to me, a sense of calm resolve in her voice—a promise.

Weak light dribbles through the thin staircase windows. I lean my side against the cool concrete wall, close my eyes. The darkness is filled with sounds: the hum of fluorescent lights, a siren pulling away from the parking lot, the buzz-pull of a fax machine from the offices above. I breathe through them, and know I'm where I'm supposed to be. Where I want to be.

My phone buzzes in my pocket. I open the message from Yarro:

Tell me about it over coffee. I have tomorrow off.

I type a reply, and return the phone to my pocket. Elation begins to bubble up in my chest, and I channel it to the task ahead. I crest the stairs and stride towards the "Special Operations" office.

"Come on in, Nan," Agent Alard calls through the open door. Inside, the light from the windows is fading, and the overhead fixture doesn't do much besides cast shadows. The desk, on the other hand, is illuminated by a warm orange lamp; Agent Alard is completely visible on the other side of it, his long hair glowing, her posture relaxed.

Once I'm settled in one of the wooden chairs, Agent Alard gets to business. "I've discussed many of the details with Adam and Jessica about the events leading up to Reena's death." Agent Alard keeps eye contact, their drooping lid reminding me of Adam's constantly tired expression. "But I am particularly interested in how you came to be involved with this family at all. You're not related, correct?"

"Not by blood," I say, a smile finding its way to my face as I remember my initial reaction to the Fit family.

Agent Alard nods in understanding. "I'm going to make some notes as we go along. If you need a break or don't want to answer something, you just let me know."

I take a deep breath. "I'm ready." My eyes focus on the bookshelf behind Agent Alard and I find a place to begin.

CHAPTER FORTY
Being

ADAM LEAVES US at the door of the police station. Jessica and I drive back to the apartment in the borrowed Jeep. We climb the metal stairs in silence.

It's late, well after sunset. The fold-out cot under the art wall is a relief. I sit on the quilted duvet that Jessica gave me when I started sleeping here.

Jessica takes off her trench coat and hangs it on the rack. She wears the same black sweater and jeans that she's been wearing for the past three days. Her white, flyaway hair is lank and tired; her eyelids and mouth droop. She pauses for a moment over her hiking boots, and decides to keep them on. Passing me with a nod, she slides open the patio door and steps outside.

I'm worn out from talking to Agent Alard. Now that I've gone over the story of the past few weeks, there's so much to work through—so many questions. Telling it has given me a new version of Reena that I want to apologise to, but can't reach. Her shadowed meditation corner waits, an open invitation.

Instead, I follow Jessica on to the patio. Grey moonlight filters through the thick blanket of clouds reflecting the orange glow from downtown. Shadowed outlines of apartment blocks and skyscrapers hulk in the distance, thousands of yellow and white eyes embedded in their metal-concrete bodies.

Jessica holds onto the railing, stretching back from it, head down. Green tiles show through the thin film of snow where her boots have disturbed it. She straightens as I slide the glass door closed.

Joining her, I lean my elbows on the railing, glad that my feet are insulated in my shoes. Spring may be around the corner, but the air is still sharp, the wind icy. That's all the reminder of Reena I need. I push down tears.

"How are you doing?" I ask instead.

"Terrible," Jessica grunts, directing her anger at the cloud cover.

"Yeah."

"Meeting with Agent Alard was important," she continues after a moment. "I know that. But it's hard to believe that it's going to make a difference. Marius and his ilk are out there, right now, hurting people and getting away with it. Was Amber another victim? There was so much more I should have done. And even if they catch the man responsible for—" A shiver passes across Jessica's sweatered shoulders.

"It won't bring Reena back," I venture.

She crosses her arms. "I'm going to get justice for Reena, and everyone else those men have hurt. I just…don't know how yet." Her eyes go glassy. "I don't know what to do."

"'Do without doing'," I remember. "What Reena used to say, right? Like water, affecting the world by being ourselves?"

Jessica blinks a couple times and relaxes her hands back down onto the railing. A gust sweeps across the street, carrying an updraft of stray snowflakes that drift against our legs.

"I wish you could've gotten to know her better," Jessica says.

"Me too."

She fishes something from her jeans pocket and holds it out to me, secure between her thumb and pointer finger.

It's a key.

"This one sticks a bit, but it works. You're welcome here—any time you want, for as long as you want."

"Really?" I hesitate. "I caused you so much trouble...I could've..."

"Not your fault." She holds the key steady. "You got thrown into this situation, this family, and even though there's no reward, no reason, you keep showing up for us."

"That's what family is, right?" I say, wanting so much to call this place home, at the same time so afraid of fucking it up.

For the first time in a long time, Jessica's mouth forms into a smile. "Being there for each other. As best as we can."

I take the apartment key.

"Thank you."

Her nod is heavy, the weight of the day finally slowing her down. The orange glow from the city illuminates her sharp features. She shivers as another gust of wind screams through the alley.

"It's cold," I run a hand back and forth across her back. "Come on."

I slide open the door and wait for her.

Jessica turns from the city, an exhale obscuring her face. When it clears, she's there, full of life and grief and fierce generosity. Shadows and city light flow over her as she carves her way across the patio.

She is here, in the present. And somewhere in the city, so are Adam and Mr. Snaff and my mom and Sid and Yarro. And so am I.

For now, that's the only answer I need.

ACKNOWLEDGMENTS

I am indebted to the first writer's group I brought this book to, who stuck with it week by week, chapter by chapter. My deepest thanks to Amilcar John Nogueira, Kate Hargreaves, Gwen Aube, and Cael Dobson.

Many thanks to the Windsor Arts, Culture, and Heritage Fund for providing the finances and deadlines I needed to finish the latter half of this book. The grant also gave me the opportunity to interview ten people about their experiences with body and gender. I am so grateful for their kind insights and the chance to meaningfully engage with the Windsor community.

Thank you to my first editor Hanan Hazime, who handled a very fragile first draft with so much care. Your genuine enthusiasm and exceptional notes were so appreciated!

I'm also thankful for the support of the Writers' Federation of Nova Scotia. The Novel Intensive facilitated by Stephanie Domet got me back on track for the final version of this book. Thanks to all of the workshop participants for your amazing feedback!

All hail Little Ghosts Books! You are the perfect home for this weird little novella. Thank you so much to Chris ! for your insightful edits, and for always answering my anxious emails with steadfast support and enthusiasm. I'm so grateful to everyone who had a hand in putting this book together.

To the Writing Wrecking Crew: Ben Van Dongen, C.M. Forest, and Elly Blake—I can't overstate how much your friendship and encouragement have meant to me over the past five years. Thank you for believing in me.

Gratitude to my dear friends who are always up for writing chats—Nico VC, Zach Supina, Cecilia Miller, Cass Caron, Aaron Daigle, Elizabeth J. M. Walker, Alexander Zelenyj, Jasper Appler, Joanna Kimmerly-Smith, Michelle Heumann, Lydia Friesen, Shawna Diane Partridge, and Cindy Chen.

A shoutout to my Ko-fi supporters, especially Sarah K, Sam G, and Owen S! Thanks for journeying with me on this long creative road.

My family is a part of who I am and I'm always grateful for their support. Thank you to my Mom, my Dads, my sister, my in-laws, my extended family, and my cats.

And thanks to Peter—my first reader, my deep listener, my love. You always know which song to play.

AUTHOR BIO

Brittni Brinn (she/they) writes from a tower and sometimes a cottage in Mi'kma'ki/Nova Scotia. She holds a M.A. in Creative Writing from UWindsor, and worked in community theatre for several years. Their interests include rocks kicked up by the ocean, books from friends, and comfortable sweaters.

Read more at brittnibrinn.com

LIST OF WORKS BY BRITTNI BRINN

The Patch Project Series (Adventure Worlds Press)
The Patch Project
A Place That Used to Be
Where Long Shadows End

Short Stories
"Gull in the Storm" in *Sunshine Superhighway: Solar Sailings* (JayHenge Publishing)

"For Your Safety and Comfort" in *Your Flight Has Been Cancelled* (Little Ghosts Press)

"Safe Passage" in *At the Lighthouse* (Eibonvale Press)

"Field Notes from the Unknown Planet" in *Far, Far Away: 7 Stories in 7 Realms of Science Fiction and Fantasy* (Mirror World Publishing)